DOLPHIN SONG

DOLPHIN SONG

•

Wilma Fasano

AVALON BOOKS
NEW YORK

PRINTED IN THE UNITED STATES OF AMERICA
ON ACID-FREE PAPER
BY HADDON CRAFTSMEN, BLOOMSBURG, PENNSYLVANIA

To my dear granddaughters, Lauren and Maggie.
I hope that when you are older, you will enjoy reading this book,
and that some day you too will have the chance to visit the wild
dolphins of West Australia.

Chapter One

So—Digger Coady had returned to Los Angeles.

Cass Chase sat back in her black imitation-leather recliner and closed her eyes, then returned to the newspaper. "Lecture on dolphins," she read. "The wild dolphins of Dolphin Bay. Visiting lecturer. Jack 'Digger' Coady, from Australia."

There was a sudden ache in her throat.

Digger Coady was here, in Los Angeles. After six years, he had come, as he came every night in her dreams, across the Pacific from Australia. She stared at the newspaper until the print blurred and pulsated in fuzzy waves.

He would be thirty now. He was just four years older than she was.

Six years ago, they'd been an item—Cassandra

Chase and Digger Coady. He'd wanted her to marry him, to go home with him to Australia. What would he want of her now?

The red light of her coffee percolator winked, and the rich aroma of coffee pulled her back to the world of here and now. Robot-like, she moved from the recliner to the kitchen.

The mug she selected was one Digger had given her. The words on one side read, *Aussie men are better kissers*. On the other side was a sketch of a person shaped like a flying saucer and topped by a fatuous grin.

Obviously, the artist had never seen Digger—Digger with his lean body and his sunlit smile.

As Cass lifted the coffeepot, she was mirrored in its stainless-steel exterior, polished so highly it looked like chrome. The curved surface distorted her image, giving her slender body and the perfect oval of her face the same warped, flying-saucer shape of the figure on the mug. The polished metal reflected with perfect clarity her deep tan, her golden eyes, framed by rich brown brows and lashes, and her blond hair, darker and shorter than it had been six years ago.

Cass poured her coffee and curled her cold hands around the warmth of the mug as she leaned against the counter, cherishing the smell of the rich brew as it mingled with the sharp clean scents of floor wax and furniture polish. This one-bedroom condo was her sanctuary. She was a private person, and after the bustling dorms of her university years, and her daily travel on crowded city buses, she thought of it as a haven of peace.

Like a small child circles the house after an absence, patting all the toys, she wandered through the living areas, touching each treasured possession as if its very existence, and her own, had been threatened. She stroked the black glass dishwasher, ran one finger lovingly around the rim of a crimson plate, caressed the smooth white countertop and cupboards.

She moved from the black and white tiles of the kitchen floor onto the pale gray carpet of the living room. She stroked the folds of the scarlet drapes that she had sewn herself, and ran her hand lightly across the velvety tops of the off-white loveseat and easy chair. Her touch lingered on the smooth off-white surfaces of the coffee table and end tables that she had bought second-hand, and sanded and painted with tender loving care.

This home was small, but it was quiet, and it was hers. She'd worked hard to save the down payment so that she could buy this condo. If Digger had come for her, could she give this up? Could she trade this hard-won sanctuary for the red sands of Australia—give up a job she loved for the uncertainty of a foreign land?

She lit the gas fireplace and sat down on the loveseat with a second cup of coffee.

She'd just returned from the small dolphinarium where she worked. It was early April, and she had become chilled through and through, wearing a top-hat and majorette's boots and a red-sequined swimsuit, standing outdoors putting two dolphins through their paces for the Sunday afternoon crowd.

Now that she was back in her apartment, snug and secure, Digger had come to haunt her, to disturb her security, to take her into the unknown.

She finished her coffee and put down the mug, then propped her chin on her clasped hands and stared into the fireplace. Even worse, maybe he hadn't. Maybe his being here had nothing to do with her. He might not want her any more. She might not want him any more. If she saw him again, maybe her dreams of him would disappear. He might be bald, fat, have an ugly wife and six ugly kids.

Maybe he would look like the figure on the coffee mug.

She had to find out. If she didn't go, she couldn't exorcise him. The ad in the paper gave the time and place of the lecture. If she looked at him as at a stranger, she could slip out quietly when it was over.

What if she still cared for him, but he no longer cared for her? Six years had gone by with no message from him.

Six years ago, they had spoken of love, but now she wondered if she'd been too young to really understand the word. Had she had a post-teenage crush on some-one whom she saw as handsome and exotic?

She'd take the chance of going to see him tonight. She had to know.

She changed into black flare-leg pants with a black stretch-top T-shirt and a turquoise chenille cardigan that set off the golden tones of her hair and skin and eyes. Then she ran for the bus.

She reached her destination with little time to spare and rushed through the doors and down the darkened aisle, slipping into a front seat just as he began.

"G'day, mates," he said, "I'm Digger Coady, from Dolphin Bay, Australia." He pronounced *Australia* almost as if it were spelled *Austrilia*, with a long *i*. "Actually, my name is Jack. *Digger* is a nickname, an Australian term, just like we might call an American in my country *Yank*."

He went on, "I'm here, formally, on behalf of our tourism agencies to encourage you to visit our beautiful country, and, informally, on behalf of the many organizations fighting to preserve our environment and our wildlife. I want to impress upon you how we have to change our ways if the beautiful creatures that share our world are still going to be around ten or twenty years from now.

"I'm here tonight to talk to you about dolphins."

He talked without notes, without a lectern to hide behind. He talked comfortably, casually, as he would have conversed with friends.

Cass drank in his appearance and listened to his accent, almost indistinguishable from British speech to an American ear. It was Digger, her Digger, no doubt of that. Many times in the lonely nights, after she had awakened from her dreams, she had wondered if she'd made the right choice when she'd refused to marry him and go to Australia.

She couldn't give up her education, she'd told him. Getting a degree in marine biology had been a hard-fought battle with part-time jobs and scholarships. She couldn't quit when she was so close to finishing.

Looking at him now, she wondered again if she'd made the right choice. His blond hair was lighter than she remembered, probably bleached by being outdoors in the sun day after day. His eyebrows and lashes were almost white, set off by the bronzed tones of his lean face. He looked out over the crowd with blazing blue eyes.

Tonight he was dressed in a dark suit, white shirt, and tie. He was not bald, nor fat, nor ugly. It was highly unlikely that any wife or kids would be fat or ugly. His shoulders were even broader than she'd remembered and his waist and hips even leaner. If she'd come here for a cure, she hadn't been successful.

She turned her attention to his words. He worked as a ranger in West Australia at a place called Dolphin Bay, where wild dolphins came into the shallow water to play with the people. Dolphin Bay was located hundreds of miles north of Perth, and surrounded by desert.

Dolphins, Digger said, had always been identified

with man. There were early myths about dolphins be-
friending men and even of men riding on the backs of
dolphins. Modern man had long considered these
myths as just that, myths, but now that dolphins were
being studied seriously and as more modern reports of
contacts came in, the experts were re-evaluating some
of the ancient stories.

"Well," he said, as he ended the lecture, "tourists
certainly cannot ride the wild dolphins of Dolphin
Bay, but they can and do become friends with them,
if only for a morning."

Then he showed slides, projected from his laptop
computer, by way of a microprojector, to a screen on
the stage. The dolphins that Cass worked with were
old and tame and carefully trained. These slides
showed wild dolphins, sleek and free and lovely,
greeting their human friends as equals, meeting them
in the shallow water, the neutral territory dividing the
sea, which belongs to the dolphins, from the earth,
which belongs to man.

Tourists fed fish to the dolphins and were rewarded
by having the animals swim close enough to be patted.
It was, Digger said, like patting a wet inner tube, but
much more satisfying. There seemed to be a rapport
that flashed between dolphin and human.

Cass forced herself to concentrate on the slides: the
azure sea, the long jetty, the beach of golden sand, and
the pelican cruising along the shore, the wedge of
black feathers going from his back to his tail over-

lapping the white feathers so perfectly that he looked like a paint-by-number picture. The dolphins, slim and beautiful with their slate-gray, torpedo-like bodies, swam and smiled and reached for fish. The tourists, bent over with their fish, waited to be singled out and blessed by a dolphin.

Cass glanced away from the slides to Digger's face, then looked back at the slides. She couldn't bear looking at Digger—so golden, so lean, so exciting. What if he were married? She forced her gaze down onto her hands.

The slides were over. Digger closed with another appeal for conservation of the dolphins and all wild creatures. Then he placed brochures on the table by the side of the stage. These gave information about Australian tourism and about organizations dedicated to protecting the environment.

Cass patted her hair nervously, took a deep breath, and walked down the aisle and onto the stage. People crowded the stage, talking to Digger, asking him questions about the dolphins and about Australia. Cass hung back at the edges of the crowd, waiting for him to be alone.

Slowly the others drifted off, and Digger began to pack up his laptop and the remaining brochures.

She took another deep breath, walked toward him, and said, with an effort at being casual, "G'day, mate. Could I shout you a drink?"

He turned from his boxes and looked at her, puzzled

for a moment, recognizing the Australian words with-out the accent that should go with them.

Then he exclaimed, "Cass!"

"Yes. Your favorite sheila. Remember?"

She opened her arms and went to him, embracing him and kissing him. It was the kiss of old friends meeting, a kiss that he would have no problem ex-plaining to a wife if one were standing backstage in the shadows. It was a carefully orchestrated kiss, a kiss that said, *If you're unavailable we're old friends, but if you are available . . .*

She stood on tiptoe, hugging him, nestling her cheek against his. He held her tightly for a moment, then moved her to arms' length, his hands still grasping her upper arms.

"You came," he said, with wonder in his voice, then, "Oh, Cass, it's good to see you. But you've changed somehow." It was all right, she thought. He'd forgiven her for rejecting him. She ran her thumbs over the muscles of his forearms, remembering the times when his arms were bare, not covered by a long-sleeved shirt and a suit jacket. She forced her hands to go still.

"Oh," she said, "I've cut my hair, and let it go back to its natural color. I used to bleach it, you know."

"Yes," he said, "I know. I remember. It used to smell like lemons." He leaned toward her and breathed in deeply. "Ah," he said, "it still smells like lemons."

He reached up with one hand and traced the contours of her face. Her jaw was a bit too wide, and her chin a bit too pointed for beauty. She knew that. His hand moved to caress her hair, now the tawny color of a lion's pelt, parted on the left with long bangs swept to the right side. It was cut in front to come just below her ears, and turned under slightly on the ends. She wore plain gold earrings.

"A golden girl," Digger said huskily, his hand cupping the back of her head, caressing the turned-under ends of her hair. "Your hair, your eyes, your skin, all a tawny gold." He released her and stepped back abruptly. "I've missed you."

He turned away and unplugged the laptop from the microprojector and the microprojector from the plug-in in the wall, then began to wind up the cord.

"Here," Cass said, "I'll carry your projector for you, and you can make it in one trip."

He handed it to her.

"I've a rental car in the parking lot," he said. "We'll go somewhere for coffee."

Digger opened the car door for Cass, then moved to his own side of the car. He took off his jacket, struggled with the tie and threw them both into the back seat.

"Ah, that feels good," he said, as he undid the top buttons of his white shirt and stretched, revealing powerful muscles that rippled along the sleeves and back of the shirt.

She remembered. He'd always hated dressing up. It confined and caged him. He'd been a man of jeans and shorts, a man of open skies and empty spaces.

He unbuttoned the cuffs of his shirt, and rolled the sleeves loosely, almost to his elbows. The sun-bleached hairs on his arms and on the backs of his fingers glinted palely under the street light. Cass, watching, felt her heart give a little spasm, as if it had been touched with a low-voltage wire.

Then he was in the car beside her. "There's no one else?" he asked. "No husband? No fiancé?"

"No," she said. "Just casual dates. No one serious."

"Good," he said, and smiled.

He reached for her tentatively at first, running a thumb back and forth along her collarbone.

There is no pulse in a collarbone, she told herself.

But somehow, there was.

He moved his thumb to caress the lower edge of her jaw and throat.

"Oh, Cass," he murmured, and he reached for her with his other arm, putting it around her, drawing her into him. "Oh, Cass." He kissed her gently, then released her.

"It's been a long time," he said.

They drove to a restaurant.

"I hoped you'd see the notice in the paper and come," Digger said. "I tried the phone book. It had pages of Chases. I didn't even know if that would still be your name. I tried the first three C. Chases. One told me I had a wrong number. The second one said to bring a bottle with me and we'd have a great party. The third said that harassing phone calls were illegal and she was going to call the police."

Cass laughed. She'd remembered his kisses, but she'd almost forgotten his warm and comfortable everyday personality.

"What on earth did you say to her?"

"Would you believe 'hello'? Anyway, there didn't seem much future in going through the rest of the phone book. If you hadn't turned up tonight, tomorrow I was going to get in touch with some of the profs at the university and see if any of them knew what had become of you."

She smiled. "No big mystery. I stayed here and got a job. I'll tell you about it in awhile."

"It's been a long six years, Cass," Digger said. "I was smarting from injured pride at first, but then it occurred to me that we both might have grown up a bit. It was unfair to expect you to drop everything you'd worked for and romp off to a foreign country. But I thought it wouldn't hurt to see if we still have anything in common."

Her pulse leapt and her heart began to race. The light in his eyes changed to blue flame. Their cups of coffee and plates of fries remained untouched, as Cass and Digger sat across from each other in the booth, leaning forward on their elbows, breathing in the reality of each other. Their hands touched and investigated, each finger poignant with its own memories.

There was no doubt he was delighted to see her again. It was in his voice, his eyes, his touch.

Finally he spoke, and, as they explored hands, a torrent of words was unleashed.

"Do you remember?' he asked. "Do you remember the day we first met? You'd been given permission to take a graduate class and fate sat us together."

She grinned. "It wasn't fate. It was the prof. He used alphabetical seating and there wasn't anyone between Chase and Coady."

Digger shrugged. "Well, that was fate, wasn't it? There could have been Chisolm and Cinbar, and, oh, lots of things."

Cass chuckled. "Right. But, yes, I remember. You called me a sheila, and I thought you had me mixed up with another girl."

"And then I told you, a sheila was just a girl and a bloke was a fellow, and then I told you—"

"Oh, yes," she said, breathless, "that you were Digger Coady from Australia. You pronounced your name *Diggah*."

"Go on," he said, laughing. "You know very well you were the one who talked funny."

"Do you remember the stories you used to tell about the kangaroos teasing the farm dogs?"

"Do you remember the prof who filled his swim-

14   *Wilma Fasano*

ming pool with ocean water and kept a dolphin in it? We used to take turns bringing it fish?"

"Do you remember you gave me opals for Valentine's Day, and took me out and we danced all night?"

They both fell silent and reached for their coffee cups.

Cass broke the silence first. "Do you remember the day we were going to Disneyland, and I came down with the flu, and you made chicken soup and brought it over to the dorm in a thermos?"

"We never did get to Disneyland, did we? We'll do it tomorrow. Do you remember the day I graduated, and we picked up my regalia, and you put it on and clowned in it? It was the size of an elephant and you were the size of a mouse."

He was six-two, she remembered. "Go on," she said. "I'm only eight inches shorter than you."

"And then you insisted on putting it on me, standing on your tiptoes."

"I was so proud of you that day," she said. "You looked so distinguished in it, the day you graduated with your master's."

Nobody said the next "Do you remember?" There was a silence as they both remembered what had happened next. In the uncomfortable stillness that followed, they turned back to their half-empty cups of cold coffee.

He was here. He had come to find her. She couldn't let him go again.

"I'm sorry, Digger," she said. "It was wrong to hurt you, but I'd worked so hard for my education. I just couldn't give it up."

"It's all right," he said. "I understand now. You were very young. I was young. We'll have both grown up and changed. You have your education now."

With one hand she toyed with her coffee cup so that the coffee swirled in it. With the other, she reached out and teased the hairs on the backs of his hands.

When they began to talk again, they skirted the *do you remembers* and talked of the trivia of the here and now.

She brought him up to date on her life. After she graduated, she told him, she got this job with a marina and small dolphin show. She was the only employee—secretary, inventory clerk, small engine mechanic, animal feeder, and four times a week she dressed up like a circus clown and literally put two trained dolphins through hoops.

"Your dolphins seem much more interesting," she said.

She touched his hand lightly and leaned forward. "Tell me more about them."

She listened raptly as he told her about the dolphins of Dolphin Bay.

He talked about them as if they were members of his family. There had been as many as eighty different ones, he said, that had appeared at one time or another, some only once. There were a smaller number that visited frequently. Then there were the ones that came nearly every day.

These had names, and could be recognized by different sizes, scars, shapes, personalities—just like people.

Old Scarface was the matriarch of the group. Three of the adults that came regularly were her children.

The youngest of these was Bugsy, an adolescent son. He was just like many human adolescent males—surly, and selfish, and rude. When tourists came into the water, he would swim between them and the other dolphins, reaching angrily for the fish. Then when he had the fish secure, he'd refuse to be petted and would swim away. On occasion he had snapped at people who tried to touch him, and the rangers warned people against him. In a tourist operation, he would have been fenced away from the people, but here in the wild he could go where he chose.

Old Scarface also had two daughters, Darby and Joan. Darby had a new baby, which she brought into the bay nearly every day.

The rangers named it Bubbles, because it was bright and lovely and effervescent. Darby and Bubbles were favorites with the crowd, but Darby, although she brought Bubbles in every day, always swam between her and any tourist who reached out to pet her.

"Tell me about some of the incidents that have happened," Cass said.

He told her of the time little Bubbles had a tin can

caught on her beak. Jagged pieces of metal hung down into the can so that the harder Bubbles tried to remove the can, the more firmly it became stuck and the more painfully it jabbed her.

Darby had brought her to the beach. It was evening and the bay was deserted. Darby cavorted and squeaked and squealed and slapped the water to get attention.

Digger, working late in his office with the window open, finally heard the commotion. He came down onto the beach, and Darby nosed little Bubbles toward him, through the water.

He examined the can. He knew that trying to pull it off would only drive the jagged triangles of metal deeper. All the time, Darby hovered anxiously.

Digger reached over Bubbles and scratched Darby's beak. "It's okay, old girl," he'd said. "I'll take care of your baby for you, but I have to get some tools first."

When he left the beach, Darby cried and squealed, frantic with despair, until he returned with tin snips.

All the time he cut at the can, Darby made dolphin noises, telling Bubbles, he supposed, to be still and let the nice man help her. Anyway, Bubbles remained very still until the can was finally removed.

He examined the beak for damage and decided that Bubbles would be fine. He slapped her gently on the side, and she turned away. Darby came up to him and touched him delicately with the end of her beak, as if to say, "Thank you!"

"You're welcome, old girl," he'd replied, and she had jumped out of the water, celebrating in sheer joy, and then moved out into the deep water to go about the business of finding fish.

"And that's the story of Darby and Bubbles," Digger said. "I've been talking a long time. What about your work? You've just heard all about my dolphins. Tell me about yours."

He leaned toward her, across the table. Cass breathed deeply to steady her voice.

"We've had the same dolphins a long time," she said. "Carl—my boss—got them from a fisherman who kept his boat in the marina. He was a kind man, and had caught these dolphins in his net. They'd been injured thrashing around, and he wasn't sure it was okay to just throw them back. Carl nursed them back to health and that was the start of The Dolphins' Dive. Carl's dad had died recently and Carl had just retired from the navy and taken over the marina. He'd worked with dolphins when he was in the navy, and was fascinated by them. When these two fell into his lap, he got the idea for the dolphin show. He started to train them. For the first few years his wife, MaryAnne, was the public performer. But then MaryAnne decided she wanted to have babies and stay at home with them."

Cass shrugged lightly. "They advertised for someone. I'd just graduated, and I wanted to work with dolphins so I applied. And that's why I get dressed up in a sequined swimsuit, just like an organ-grinder's monkey, and put the dolphins through their paces."

"Well," Digger said, "it wouldn't be my cup of tea, but I suppose it's a job. And I don't imagine I can even get too moralistic about your dolphins. They probably would have died, or in their weakened state been caught by sharks. I imagine jumping after colored balls is better than being eaten by a shark."

Cass ignored the unspoken but insinuated *but not much*. He'd just been too polite to say the words.

She continued, "I don't know what the next few years will bring. The show is in trouble. The big oceanariums draw most of the crowds. The dolphins in our little show are getting old. Their names are Snick and Snee, by the way. They're really sweethearts, but, as you know, dolphins in captivity age much more rapidly."

"I'm sure you're right about that."

"We treat them very well," she said defensively. "They're never abused. They're well fed. They don't have to worry about sharks or nets. We don't overwork them. Both Carl and I know enough about dolphins to know they're very susceptible to stress, so we have only four shows a week—Friday and Saturday evening, Sunday afternoon, and one on Wednesday morning. That one is generally attended by regulars— senior citizens and young mothers with preschoolers. The senior residences often bring busloads of seniors.

"So you see," she said wryly, "we do spread happiness in our own little way."

He rolled his coffee cup stiffly between his palms, which were held straight and parallel. "I know, Cass," he said, "but I still prefer mine wild."

"Yes, I suppose so," she said and changed the subject.

"What are your plans for this trip?" she asked. "Are you staying in Los Angeles long? Where are you going when you finish here?"

"I'm spending another week in LA," he said. "I have just one more lecture to give here, on Friday evening, but until then I'm going to take a few days off to be a tourist. Do I hear an offer for guiding services?"

"Yes," she told him. "Yes, you do. Monday and Tuesday are my regular days off, because of the fact that I work weekends, but I think that if I talk to Carl, he'll probably give me the rest of the week too, except for the shows. I haven't had a vacation for a long time."

It had gone wrong, she thought. The magic had left the evening. They'd become two strangers talking across a table. But she still had nearly a week to make things right.

They walked to the car in silence and drove through the streets in silence.

He stopped the car in front of her apartment. "I'd better give you my number, just in case." He scribbled

the name and number of his hotel on one of the brochures piled on the back seat and handed it to her.
"I'll pick you up in the morning," he said, "because
tomorrow we're going to have that day in Disneyland."

Chapter Two

Digger drove back to his hotel.

She had come. He'd seen her again, this young woman he'd known six years ago. She'd broken his heart then with her refusal to become his wife and move to Australia. For months, he'd been hurt and angry, too hurt to write or phone.

But, he assured himself, he'd grown up. Looking at things rationally, he could no longer blame her for not ditching everything and rushing off with him to an unknown continent.

By the time his anger and his hurt had gone, so much time had passed that he felt foolish trying to contact her. She was an episode in his past, water under the bridge, ships that pass in the night, whatever clichés dealt with relegating a woman who breaks your heart to the empty bygone pages of your life.

He was older now, and wiser. Recently, memories of her had niggled at him, her enthusiasm, her joy, her love of dolphins, to say nothing of the way his heart raced when he kissed her. Maybe there had been something there worth salvaging—at least worth re-exploring.

When this promotional trip came up, he'd snatched the opportunity. This time, he wouldn't rush into a proposal. He'd meet her as a friend. If embers still smoldered under the ashes of the past, he'd take things slowly, be sure of both of them before he fanned the embers into flame by blurting out rash offers of marriage.

For now, one day at a time.

Next morning, Cass got on the bus. If she wanted to spend most of the week with Digger, she needed the time off, and she preferred to ask in person rather than by phone. Carl, her boss, would give her the time. She knew that. She had weeks and weeks of unused vacation coming, and Carl was a very considerate boss.

Carl Jorgensen was in his early fifties, tall and angular, and unusually dark for a Swede. His pock-marked complexion and black handlebar moustache gave him the swarthy look of a pirate. Except for his coloring he looked the stereotype of an ancient Viking, but he was kind-hearted.

He could afford to be. The dolphin show was his hobby. The marina brought in the money. Also, he owned twenty acres of beachfront property to the south of Los Angeles, a veritable gold mine.

He'd been almost forty when he married a pretty girl nearly twenty years his junior. They'd lived happily ever after and he was still devoted to her, the dark, petite wife named MaryAnne, and to their two plump preschoolers. Occasionally Cass offered to stay with the children for an evening while Carl and MaryAnne went out.

Cass reached the marina at eight-thirty, relieved to be off the crowded bus. Once inside the office, she brewed a pot of coffee.

The office building was simply an addition to Carl's house, with a door that opened directly into the kitchen. The main room of the office was clean but cluttered, with an old desk and an older filing cabinet, fishing gear, buckets, and props for the dolphin shows. There was a second room, scrupulously neat, where Cass kept her costumes and changed for the shows. The computer system shared a corner of this.

Carl appeared in the office, dressed in old jeans and a workshirt, as soon as he heard her come in.

"What's up?" he asked. "Isn't this your day off?"

She cradled her cup.

"I came to ask a favor. Why don't you just go back and get your coffee cup?"

He disappeared, and returned two minutes later with a coffee mug, already a quarter filled with real cream. He filled the rest of the cup with coffee, and sat down behind his office desk, feet up, chair tipped back.

"Okay. Run it by me."

"Well, last night I ran into an old friend. He's in town for a few days, so I wondered if I could have some time off."

"Cass," Carl said, "you have only to ask. You know that. Give me a call when you know exactly which days you're going to be away."

She set down her cup. "Thanks," she said. "Starting today, but I'll take care of the mail first."

"Never mind the mail. You think I don't know how to open an envelope. Just get on the next bus and have a good time."

"I'll still do the shows, and he'll probably come, at least to one of them."

"Good. You just show your young man Disneyland or whatever. I'll see you for the Wednesday morning show." He added, "And I want to be introduced, so I can pass judgement on him. After all, I'm the closest thing to a father you've got out here."

Digger appeared promptly at one o'clock. By then, Cass had showered, dried her hair, eaten lightly, and was dressed in walking shorts of red and black tartan with a black turtleneck sweater. Over it she wore a bright red cable-knit sweater to keep out chill winds.

Digger wore khaki shorts and a white sweatshirt.

He looked approvingly at her neat white sneakers. Touring Disneyland would involve miles of walking. "Nice socks," he said. They were trimmed with a narrow band of the same tartan material as her shorts.

"You like them? I had some material left over after I finished the shorts."

"You made those? You sew?"

She grinned at him. "I make all my own clothes," she said. She added, "I'm a gourmet cook too. And I've taking up serious running. I've acquired all sorts of talents since you last saw me. All I did then was study."

He grinned back. "And go out with me."

They drove to Anaheim, Cass relishing the ride along the freeways, in a car with one handsome man, rather than on a crowded bus full of fellow commuters. Maybe before long, she'd save enough money for a car of her own.

They read the sign welcoming them to the park.

"To us," Digger said. "To us, and to all the wonderful things that sign promises us."

Disneyland was not crowded. It was a weekday and not one of the various spring breaks.

Digger bought Cass a red balloon to match her sweater. She clutched it firmly, as they rode around the park on the steam-powered train that encircles Disneyland.

They walked down Main Street, enjoying the world of yesterday, its shops and old fire engines and marching bands. They rode the white horses of an old-fashioned carousel, and they boarded the riverboat and wandered hand-in-hand over Tom Sawyer's island, reluctant to leave.

They took the rides and tramped the streets, and ate from the street vendors. They toured tomorrow on Space Mountain, and viewed make-believe animals; they plummeted down the side of Splash Mountain; they whistled through the ice caves and past the monster with the glowing eyes that lived on the Matterhorn.

As evening fell, they cruised in a pirate ship amongst the Pirates of the Caribbean, and finally ate a leisurely meal in the Blue Bayou.

Digger took pictures of her everywhere: on the rides, on Tom Sawyer's island, shaking hands with Mickey and Goofy, on Main Street clutching her red balloon. Pictures to show back home, he said, back home in Australia. A pang of emptiness stabbed Cass, as she thought of the family at the lonely ranch looking at these pictures of the young woman they would probably never meet.

What would they think of her if they did meet her, if Digger were to take her home to them?

* * *

"Would you like to come in for coffee?" Cass said later as they stood in the hallway in front of her condo.

"Yes. Yes, I would."

While coffee perked, Cass turned on the gas fireplace, then disappeared into the bedroom to change. She dressed in slim black velvet pants with a gold-tasseled belt, and an ivory silk shirt that shimmered. Digger, six years ago, had given her an opal pendant with matching drop earrings. She put them on now, the opals with red flames of fire that flickered in every change of light. The pendant was on a gold chain.

She returned to find Digger pacing the room like something caged. She poured their coffees, Digger's with milk and hers black, and set them on the coffee table.

"Do you want to sit on the floor?"

"Sure," he said. "Why not?"

She arranged red throw cushions on the gray carpet in front of the fireplace.

Once he was seated, he held out his hand for hers and pulled her down beside him.

They sat side by side, cross-legged on the carpet, and drank coffee in silence and stared into the fire.

"You know, Cass," Digger said finally, "I handled it all wrong last time. You were too young. I had no business encouraging you to drop out of school before you finished. I shouldn't have pressured you to marry me. Let's start over. I'm not asking you to marry me now. We don't even know each other any more. We're different people. Let's just tourist together a few days, have fun, see what happens. Then maybe you could come out to Australia on vacation. Not drop your life and burn your bridges like I asked you to last time, but just come out for vacation. No commitments on either side. You want to do that?"

So she'd just been offered a second chance. Maybe. No commitment on either side. If she went on vacation to Australia to decide at the end of it that what she'd felt six years ago had been puppy love, that was fine. But what if that wasn't how she felt? What if she decided she really wanted to marry Digger, but he didn't ask her?

"Problem with money? I'll buy your ticket."

"No," she said. "I've got the money. I just have to think about it a while, talk to Carl about an extended vacation. There's no point going for only a week."

"You have vacation days coming?"

She sighed. "Yes," she said. "Enough for six vacations. I like the job and I haven't taken many days off. But I don't know if I should leave MaryAnne to do that many shows on her own."

"MaryAnne?"

"Carl's wife. She did it before he hired me, and she still enjoys getting back to it once in a while. But she has two young children now. I'm not sure how she'd like having to do every show for three or four weeks."

"Okay, Cass. I won't pressure you. We'll have fun

as if we're just getting acquainted. We won't mention it again until this week's over. Okay?"

She sighed and reached out with one hand and lay it across his back.

"Okay," she said. "Want to come running with me tomorrow morning?"

Cass had hoped to impress Digger with her running skills, but it seemed almost as if he were running at half throttle, deliberately holding himself back so as not to out-distance her.

He was in good shape, better shape than she was. He seemed to be made of steel. Yet underneath, he was tender and gentle, the gentlest person she knew. She put on an extra spurt, and effortlessly he matched it.

They had Egg McMuffins at McDonald's, and by eight-thirty were back at her apartment. She made coffee, dark and aromatic coffee, coffee for sipping leisurely while they sat cross-legged on the floor, backs supported against the loveseat, and made their plans for the day to come.

"You know," he said, "I never did get to the San Diego Zoo when I was here before. Is it worthwhile?"

She colored a bit. "I don't know," she said.

He looked at her, astonished. "You mean you've lived here forever and you've never been to the San Diego Zoo? What have you been doing with your life?"

She shrugged. "Studying. Working. Whatever. Is that what you'd like to do today?"

"Yes," he said. "I would. And I suspect you would too."

She left him looking at the map of southern California while she showered and changed out of her powder blue jogging suit, into a yellow cotton sundress, and, in case of cool breezes, a color-coordinated jacket made of a bright floral print.

They drove down the Pacific Coast Highway, slower than the freeway, but with spectacular views of sea and mountains and orange groves. They strolled through the old mission of Capistrano, the one that the swallows return to.

San Diego was warm and sunny. They wandered through the zoo, holding hands.

"Do the crocodiles make you homesick, Digger?" Cass asked, as they stood watching the heavy beasts lounging in shallow water or on a cement bank.

"Not when they're sitting on concrete," he said.

They moved on to gaze back at a gigantic turtle that was studying them across a knee-high fence.

They watched a seal show. "That's what I do," Cass said, pointing at the trainer. "But my costume's a lot more attractive. You'll come tomorrow, won't you?"

"I wouldn't miss it," he assured her. "I don't know about the costume, but the person inside it will sure be more attractive."

They moved past giraffes and polar bears and penguins, but when they reached the big eucalyptus tree with its koala, she thought that he would never move, and knew then that he was really and truly homesick, and that she'd never be able to get him to leave Australia.

"Do you want to do Sea World while we're here?"

"No," he said. "I don't think so, Cass. I like to think of dolphins as they are at Dolphin Bay." He paused. "But if you really want to, professional interest and all that, I will."

"It's all right," she said. "It would probably just depress me, like a beggar peering at Fort Knox."

On Wednesday morning, Digger dropped Cass at work at eight-thirty. It was time for her to get ready. The show started in another two hours.

She checked through her costumes. On Wednesday mornings, she usually wore something conservative. The red-sequined one-piece, on Wednesday mornings worn with a detachable short skirt, was a favorite. It was bright and glitzy. Another favorite of the seniors was her cowgirl outfit—a short fringed skirt made of black imitation leather, with a matching vest worn over a white western shirt. With that outfit, she discarded her top hat in favor of a white Stetson.

No, she thought. Not today. She would choose the smartest-looking outfit she owned. The only person in today's audience that mattered was Digger. If he had to see her in one of her ridiculous trained-monkey suits, at least he was going to see her in one that flattered her.

She chose a gold costume that looked like a one-piece swimsuit covered with gold glass beads. She had sewn those beads on herself—every one of them—by hand. Rows of golden tassels that swayed and swung with her every move dangled from both top and bottom, and there was just one tassel on each gold-painted majorette boot. The black top hat had a golden band.

After she'd finished dressing, Cass got a package of fish from the freezer and dumped it into a pail of water so it would be thawed by the time she was ready to feed it to the dolphins. Then she set the pail by the side of the pool. The performing pool looked very much like a regular swimming pool. On one side there were four rows of bleachers that would hold about a hundred people. If the crowd was larger than normal, children or young people often sat in front of the bleachers on the concrete floor. It was a far cry from a beach in West Australia.

Next she put a record of marches on the CD player and turned on the speakers above the pool. The seniors liked marches. On Friday and Saturday nights she would play rock, and on Sunday afternoon a mixture of children's music and the old-fashioned big-band sound.

While the music played and the people drifted in, she went into the tank area. She loved the atmosphere here, the strident music in the background, the sounds of the crowd gathering, the smell of saltwater coming off the bay tinged with the faint smell of fish. She loved being alone with the dolphins too. They greeted her by raising their heads out of the water. She bent down and scratched each one under his chin.

"Hi, fellas," she said. "Do a good job for me today. The honor of your country is at stake. Show him that you're just as smart as his friends at Dolphin Bay."

She slapped Snick on the side and gave Snee a rub on the beak. "And most of all, boys, show him that you're happy."

The dolphins curved around under her hands, like friendly dogs, rubbing their backs against her palms.

She released them into the pool, where they played freely until everyone was in and seated. She had thrown a couple of colored tennis balls in with them. They chased these up and down, tossing them in the air above the water with their beaks. Sometimes she felt that the crowd enjoyed this free play as much as they did the actual performance.

The music faded. Carl had turned it down. It was time for her to begin. She walked to the side of the pool, faced her audience, and picked up her mike.

"Good morning, ladies and gentlemen," she said. "I am Cassandra Chase, and for those of you who don't already know them, these are the dolphins, Snick and Snee. They enjoy performing for you, and we hope you enjoy their performance."

The music swelled up in a crescendo, then tapered

off to the normal performance level. The sun glittered on Cass's golden beads. For a moment she stood erect, straight as a baton twirler in her golden boots and her top hat.

Are you there, Digger? She hadn't seen him, but she never looked for individuals in the crowd. She always concentrated on her own performance.

She scooped the tennis balls out with a net, then said, "Fetch," as she would to a dog, throwing a ball into each end of the pool. Snee raced toward one end, Snick toward the other, competing to see which could get back to her first with a ball.

She took the balls from them, and fed each one a fish. She handed a ball to a small child in the front row. "Here," she said, bending down to talk to him, "you throw it in." He stood wistfully, one finger in his mouth, wanting to, not knowing if he should. He looked up at his mother.

"It's all right," his mother said. "Go ahead."

He threw the ball gently, barely getting it into the water. The dolphins raced for it, Snee reaching it first. They tossed it to each other, around and around the pool.

Half a dozen four-year-olds were suddenly saying, "Me too, me too." Cass let three of them have turns, then said, "Who wants to feed the dolphins?"

Thirty or so hands waved in the air. Cass held up a fish, and the hands went down.

"Ugh," said a dainty little girl, "they eat *that*?"

"What, no takers?" Cass exclaimed, then turned to the seniors, holding up her bucket.

An elderly gentleman said, "Here, miss. I'd like to."

"One for each," she said, as she handed him two fish. "Now, if you come down here, and kneel at the edge of the pool, and hold the fish out, they'll take them right from your hand."

He took the fish, and, in his khaki walking shorts and bright floral shirt, knelt carefully at the side of the pool, and was as happy as one of the children when the dolphins swam up and took the fish he held.

Cass waited for the applause to end before continuing with her own program. The dolphins seemed to enjoy the applause too. They didn't perform just for fish.

She took the dolphins through their repertoire. She held fish high in the air, and the dolphins jumped for them. There were sighs of disgust when she held a fish in her mouth for the dolphins.

Snick and Snee jumped into the air, and wheeled in the water and changed directions, all on command. They leaped up and pulled a lever which rang a bell, and they retrieved Cass's baton when she threw it into the pool.

Then they jumped through an eight-foot hoop which she held out over the water. She had taught them to approach one from either side and jump through the hoop at the same time, meeting in the air. The hoop was very popular.

After the show, she met with Digger.

"You're very good," Digger said. He cleared his throat, "Uh, very pretty too. Think those senior ladies will ever let their husbands near this place again?"

She made a face at him, and took him inside to meet Carl. The two men sized each other up and apparently liked what they saw. She left them talking about dolphins, wild, tame, and navy, while she changed.

"You will let me cook dinner for you?" she said when they were in the car.

Digger took her grocery shopping. She shopped more expensively than usual, choosing the finest filet, the crispest Romaine lettuce, the freshest of fresh pasta. When they reached the checkout, she refused his offer to pay.

He came back with her and hovered while she got dinner ready. He cut up steak for the stroganoff and prepared lettuce for Caesar salad while she made chocolate cheesecake. He watched the pasta so it wouldn't boil over. He chilled the wine.

"I'm impressed," he said of the preparations for the meal as he stirred the bubbling stroganoff.

"You needn't be," she answered. "This is just thrown together because there isn't much time. Tuesday, my day off, is the day I usually entertain, and I spend all day preparing."

Digger looked uncomfortable. "You entertain that much?" he said. "Who do you entertain?"

She reached up and patted his cheek. "Who do you think?" She smiled. "I have a procession of handsome millionaires, all threatening to throw themselves from high buildings if I won't marry them." She deftly moved the morning newspaper and a couple of books from the table. "Don't be silly," she said. "Just friends. Carl and MaryAnne once in a while. Some of the people I went to school with. Friends I've made at my running club."

Was he jealous? Wouldn't that be nice?

Digger paced the floor and kept a watchful eye on everything while Cass went into the bedroom to change out of the blue workshirt and jeans she'd worn home from work.

She changed into a full red skirt, adorned with embroidered flowers. The skirt hung almost to her ankles. The black velvet tank top and cardigan she wore with it was ornamented with embroidered red flowers to match the skirt. The only piece of jewelry she wore was a gold charm bracelet hung with leaping dolphins.

"Smashing," Digger said when she returned. He looked down at his own jeans and casual shirt.

She smiled. "You're okay. I wear jeans to work, so I like the excuse to dress up a bit when I entertain."

And if he believes that, she thought to herself, *he probably owns a whole collection of bridges*. The truth was, she wanted to look nice for him.

She set the table with a navy-blue tablecloth, bright red plates, and plain stainless-steel cutlery. She stood back and eyed it. It looked nice. Her table-settings always looked nice.

"I just have to put the candles on," she said to Digger, "and we'll be ready to eat."

She chose bright red candleholders with navy blue candles.

"Pour the wine, will you, while I dish up?"

Digger took the bottle of chilled white wine from the fridge. "You too? You didn't used to."

"No," she said. "I still don't drink. Never did. There's a bottle of white grape juice in there for me."

After Digger had poured the drinks, they sat down and faced each other across the table.

Digger paused, as though hesitating over a toast. Would he say, *To us*?

He raised his glass. "To dolphins," he said. "To all kinds of dolphins, yours and mine, wild and trained, captive and free. May they live safe and happy in this world of ours forever."

"Yes." Cass clinked her glass of white grape juice against his wine glass. "To dolphins."

She served the salad and the stroganoff.

"Very good," Digger said.

There was a pause. "So," he continued, "how are your folks? I never met them, you know."

"They're fine. Still live near Boston. Dad still tramps the streets delivering mail. Mom still works as a nurse. Both of them are looking forward to retiring in a few years."

"Have they ever been out here?"

"Yes," she said. "They came when I graduated. They don't travel much. They're saving their money to buy a place in Florida when they retire. My sister's married and has one little boy. They live in Boston."

She passed the plate of garlic bread to him. "And yours?"

"Still on the station, uh, the ranch. My brothers have pretty well taken over. They still keep Dad busy enough to make him feel useful."

Cass felt the weight of all the things unspoken.

How will your family cope if you move to Australia?

Very well, thank you. Once you're on a plane in Boston, Australia's just another hop across the ocean from California. And how would your family welcome an American girl into their Australian family?

None of these questions and answers mattered. As Digger had said, they were different people now. If she came to Australia, it would be as a tourist for a few weeks. Then they'd see how things developed. She twisted her fingers together in her lap, then brought her hands up to the table, grasped a serving dish, and smiled brightly.

"More pasta?" she said to Digger.

Chapter Three

When the meal was over, Digger loaded the dishwasher while Cass cleared the table.

She'd acquired all sorts of talents in the last six years. Now if she'd only agree to come to Australia, so he could see how she adapted to his environment. He could never leave the dolphins and the open spaces. Not permanently.

He finished loading the cutlery, then stood and looked at her.

She was bent over the table, cutting the cheesecake.

"You can pour the coffee if you like," she said.

He reached for the two mugs already set out on the counter, stirred cream into one, then filled both from the steaming glass pot.

"We'll have coffee and dessert in front of the fire," she said.

He carried the two mugs of coffee into the living room and set hers down on the coffee table. Did she intend for them to sit together on the loveseat? The idea was tempting.

Deliberately, he moved over to the recliner, set his own mug down on the end table, and sat in the recliner. He daren't sit beside her. He'd do something foolish again like blurting out a proposal, as he had six years ago.

This time, he had to be sure, and had to be sure that she was sure. He was not a man to marry easily, only to divorce just as easily. For him, marriage, when it came, would be a lifetime commitment. There was more involved than a pretty face and tender lips.

She moved into the living room with two plates of cheesecake and slid one onto the end table beside his coffee mug. She then sat down on the loveseat, cut off a small piece of cheesecake with her fork, and lifted it to her mouth.

Digger watched her, then took a bite of his own dessert.

"Very good," he said.

"Thank you."

He began to ask her again to go to Australia for a vacation, then changed his mind. He mustn't nag her, either to wear her down until she accepted or to annoy her until she refused. He'd drop the whole subject until he was ready to leave. After all, that's what he'd told her he would do.

But she was beautiful. And intelligent. And nice. She appeared to be a really nice person. He'd watched her at the morning show. Her affection for her dolphins would be hard to counterfeit. So would her consideration for the youngest and the oldest members of her audience.

She stood up and went to the CD player. The disc she chose was one of slow waltzes. The music vibrated through Digger's mind and body. Suddenly she was before him, holding out her hand.

"Dance?"

Dancing was the last thing in the world they should do. But he couldn't refuse without appearing totally boorish. He stood and took her in his arms, at first holding her loosely. They both paid attention to the steps, exaggerating the moves, as if in a ballroom dancing contest.

It wasn't any use. He couldn't pay attention to anything with Cass in his arms.

He moved her closer to him, lowered his head so that his cheek rested against her hair. He felt her gentle breath against his neck.

This had not been a good idea. He stepped back.

"I'd better go," he said.

They walked to the door, hands touching lightly.

"Good night, Cass." He bent to touch his lips to hers. She tasted like chocolate cheesecake.

He turned abruptly, then let himself out into the hall.

"Cassandra," he said softly to himself as he walked down the hall. When he reached his car, he closed his eyes a moment, picturing her swimming with the wild dolphins, and then running to him. In his mind, she wore a beaded golden swimsuit that reflected the rays of the sun in a thousand glitters, and she ran slowly, seeming to float, as do the models in television commercials. Instead of running through flower strewn meadows, she ran across red sands, her bare feet leaving little puffs of dust behind them.

He opened his eyes, shook his head to clear it of the image, then got into his car and drove back to his hotel.

The next two days passed in a bittersweet haze. Digger had laid the ground rules. They'd just get to know each other again. No talk of love and marriage. There wouldn't be any of that unless Cass went to Australia to spend a few weeks in his environment. After that there still might not be. She didn't know.

Digger treated her with his usual unfailing courtesy and gentleness. She knew he was still attracted to her. It showed in the way he held the car door for her, in the way he caressed her hand when he held it, in the way he looked at her in the moments he didn't realize she was watching. But was there more than attraction?

She couldn't tell. Was there more on her side? She wasn't even sure of that.

All she was sure of was that they had two more days together.

They drove through the hills outside the city with stands of eucalyptus and fancy homes, and then even further out into farmland. They joined a bus tour that took them through Beverly Hills, past the mansions of the movie stars.

In Hollywood, they looked at the names of the great actors, both past and present, engraved in stars embedded in the sidewalk in the Walk of Stars, on Hollywood Boulevard. They gazed at the autographs and hand and foot prints that famous stars had pressed in cement. Later they stood on the corner of Hollywood and Vine as if waiting for the ghosts of Hollywood past to walk on by.

They laughed and ate and exchanged chaste kisses. Thursday night after dinner they went dancing, and for an hour it seemed as if the last six years had never been, that they were back at UCLA, that Digger hadn't yet proposed and she hadn't yet turned him down.

He gave his final lecture on Friday evening. She didn't go. It was the night of a dolphin show, the one with the young crowd and the rock music and the psychedelic outfit that she often wore on Friday and Saturday nights.

He picked her up after the show was over. By unspoken agreement they went back to her condo. It was his last night. The next day they would go out for brunch. Then he would drive his rented car north to San Francisco, and, unless she decided to go to Australia, he would once more be out of her life forever.

He took the key from her hand and unlocked the door, then let her precede him in.

"I'll just go change," she said.

"Don't bother. I know what you look like in jeans. I like you in jeans. Instead, why don't you light that fireplace of yours and I'll make coffee."

Lighting the gas fireplace was the work of a minute. She threw herself on the loveseat in front of it and stared into the flames. She could hear Digger in the kitchen, rummaging through unfamiliar cupboards, finding coffee and filters.

He joined her on the loveseat. "Just have to wait for the red light to come on," he said. He drummed the fingers of one hand on the arm of the sofa.

"Well, Cass," he said. "How about it? Vacation at Dolphin Bay?"

Cass picked at an imaginary tear in her jeans, scratching at the material with one fingernail. "I don't know," she said. She couldn't say anything about the money saved to buy a car. If things didn't work out in Australia, she still wouldn't have a car. But if she told him that, he'd insist on paying for her ticket.

He shrugged. "Look. It's too early to make commitments. Like I told you before, we're different people now. We have to get to know each other again.

We've made a good start on that this week, but a week's not long enough. If you don't come to Australia, there's no way we can know each other any better. You have to see me at home, where I live and where I work, to know me."

She stalled. "What's it like?" she said. "Oh, I know. You've told me about the dolphins and all of that, but what's around it? Are there any other people but a couple of rangers?"

He grinned and relaxed. He quit drumming on the arm of the loveseat and instead put one arm around her shoulders and took her hand. He ran his thumb around her fingers, massaging them.

"Well," he said, "right there, you've almost hit it, although it's a bit bigger than two rangers. We have quite a large office building where we do our bookwork and sell fish and souvenirs to the tourists and all the rest of it. Sometimes students turn up to do research and write papers. There's a long wharf that runs up the middle of the bay. On our side, boats are off limits because they might harm the dolphins. On the other side there are fishing boats and pleasure boats."

"So where do all these tourists stay? Where do you live?"

"There's what you'd call an RV park a few hundred yards inland on the other side of the road. Some come in RV's—we call them caravans—and some bring tents. Then there are also a number of on-site caravans—trailers—for rent. Many are quite large, almost like mobile homes. That's where those of us who work live, and some are rented to tourists. Lots of people like to stay for an extended period of time.

"Right now the largest one, a three-bedroom mobile home, is rented to a young couple staying a year or so, Jon and Judy Brown. He's from Boston, same as your family. They met in New Zealand a year or two ago and got married. He was a Harvard professor and a writer, but his books sold so well he quit his job. She's started writing romances, so the two of them travel and write. Great life. You'll really like them."

He seemed to assume she was coming. Well, the truth was she was really tempted to do that. At worst, she'd have had the vacation of a lifetime. And dream of Digger every night for the next six years?

"Towns?"

"There's a small town a few miles down the road. It has a post office, a store, a restaurant, and a motel. Some of the tourists stay there. Oh, yes. A garage. All the essentials, but nothing fancy. Quite a few fishermen and their families live there, a few retired ranchers, whatever. There's a school and a small hospital, one doctor and one dentist. If we need much in the way of medical care, we go to Perth."

"I see." That was as noncommittal as she could get.

"Look, Cass," Digger said, "I know we don't have a roistering social life, but you don't really care about that, do you? I've never thought of you as a party person."

She shook her head. "No, you're right about that. I suppose I'm as much at home with dolphins as I am with people. But I don't know about rural areas and small towns either. I've never done that. I grew up in Boston, and then I've lived here. I've always been around concerts and good restaurants and shopping malls. And then there's my job. Would there be jobs for me there? I don't know if I can handle leaving everything I have here."

"That's why I suggested the vacation," he said, "so you can find out some of those things. But suit yourself."

Early next morning, Cass dressed herself in her running clothes, in the powder-blue running suit that she had worn when she ran with Digger. If anything could make her feel better, it would be running. She ran down to the end of the block and then over the path that led to the park. The wind whipped her hair where it fell below her powder-blue headband and tore at her cheeks. Doggedly, she set out to run for an hour.

The running didn't produce the magic it often did, but it helped. At the very least, she thought, it would do more to hide the fact that she'd spent much of the night crying than any amount of scrubbing or makeup could. Digger must not know that she shed tears over him.

Running had always cleared her mind and helped her to make good decisions. It normally relaxed and revitalized her, but this time it didn't. She spent the hour chasing the same thoughts and doubts around and around in her mind. Should she go to Australia? If she did, would she ever come back? How could she give up the pleasant life she had built for herself in Los Angeles? How could she give up Digger? What made her think she'd end up with Digger even if she did visit Australia? What would she do for a career if she did marry Digger? When she returned from her run, she was no more refreshed than she had been when she started.

She showered and changed into a skirt and sweater.

Digger picked her up and drove her to a nice restaurant for brunch. He did all the right things—helped her from the car, opened the door for her, held her chair at the restaurant before he sat down himself.

But somehow, none of it seemed right. Apparently, they'd already said everything they had to say.

They fiddled with their white linen napkins, and walked through the buffet line. Then they picked at the food, as if neither of them were hungry.

"So where are you going next?" Cass asked in a desperate attempt to fill the silent air with sound.

"Well, north to San Francisco next," he said. "You knew that. Then I'll go up through the rest of California, and to the cities in Oregon and Washington. Across the border to Vancouver, then to Calgary, then back down into the U.S. to take a swing through the Midwest."

"I see. How long will that take?"

"Not as long as it sounds. If I have more than a couple hundred miles to drive, I'll turn in the car and fly to the next place. About three weeks or so, I guess."

"I see," Cass said again. She might as well have said *that's nice*, for all the sincerity there was in her words.

The question of whether she'd spend a vacation in Australia hung unspoken in the air. She didn't intend to bring it up. Neither, apparently, did Digger.

When they left the restaurant, they left two plates full of food behind them. He drove her to her door, and again did all the right things. He walked her into the lobby, took the key from her hand and unlocked the door for her, then bent down and touched her lips for the obligatory kiss. She reached up and cradled his face in her hands for the obligatory caress.

The interactions she had with Snick and Snee were more romantic.

Cass dressed and caught the bus as soon as Digger dropped her off. She'd do her Friday night show as usual. After all, Digger had left. Why wouldn't her life return to normal?

She walked in from the bus stop, and got the coffee perking. Within a few minutes Carl entered the office area.

"Hi," he said as she came in. "I wasn't sure whether

I'd ever see you again or not." He looked at her more closely. "You look dreadful. Is anything wrong?"

She forced herself to smile naturally. "No" she lied, then as Carl peered at her she threw herself into her office chair. Carl poured coffee for them both, then stood leaning against the filing cabinet. "Yes," she said. "Yes. He's gone back, and everything's sort of, well, sort of the way it would be if he hadn't ever come. I almost wish he hadn't."

Carl raised his eyebrows. "Quarrel?"

"No. I could handle quarrels. Indifference. Just indifference. This morning, we didn't have a thing to say to each other. I might as well have been on a casual date."

"You were nothing but a casual date? That's sure not the impression I got the day I met him. Didn't exactly feel he was indifferent to you either."

"He wanted me to go to Australia for a few weeks' vacation, but what's the point of that? He said we should get to know each other again because we aren't the same people we used to be."

"That makes sense to me," Carl said.

She gestured with both hands. "But how can I do that? I can't go that far for a few days."

"I thought you said a few weeks."

"Well, that is what he said. But I have a job. He didn't leave his job for a month to come here. Coming here was part of his job. How can I just walk out for a month or so?"

Carl laughed aloud. "Well, you'll give me a chance to learn to get along without you, because I suspect that if you go I'll never see you again."

"How can I do that? There's the job. I love it. I love Snick and Snee. Then there's my condo. It's just what I want. You know how long I lived in a bachelor apartment to get the down payment for the condo. How can I just walk away?"

Carl exhaled noisily, and had a swig of his coffee. "Look, Cass," he said, "nothing worthwhile comes without a price. My whole life changed with Mary-Anne and the kids, but I wouldn't give them up for a billion dollars. People you love are worth more than all the condos and china and furniture in the world."

"You don't want me either," she said. "Digger doesn't want me. You don't want me."

"Of course I want you, Cass. But I'm not selfish enough to keep a good employee at the risk of her own happiness. I suspect Digger wants you too, or he'd have never let you know he was here, would never have asked you to spend a month casing the joint, so to speak."

"But this morning he didn't say anything about anything except the weather and wasn't the food delicious? That was the food that neither of us ate."

"And what did you talk about?"

She ran her hands through her hair. "All right, all right," she said. "I talked about how delicious all this neglected food was."

"Look," Carl said, "why don't you just go and see for yourself, like he asked you to?"

"And the job? The dolphins? The show?"

"Cass, I can do the job. I'll get a student to help out part-time until you get back. MaryAnne can run the shows until you get back. And if you never come back, I'll get someone else full-time. Probably not for the shows. Snick and Snee are getting over the hill, and there's no point in putting them under the stress of adapting to a new handler. The shows wouldn't go on that much longer anyway."

Cass flung up her head. "You're not, uh—"

He grinned. "No. What do you think I am? I'll just retire them. Other people have dogs and cats for pets. I'll have dolphins. But I won't replace them."

He sat down in the extra chair. She flung herself sideways in her chair with one arm resting on the back and her chin propped on her hand. Carl leaned back and placed both feet on the battered desk.

"Okay," he said. "So you want to take a month off and go to Australia. That's fine. You've got lots of vacation time coming. I think you've got somewhere around two and a half or three months coming. Take a month. I'll give you another month's pay in lieu of vacation."

"But you can't—" Cass said. "You don't have to do that."

He shrugged. "Why not? If you never come back, I'd have to pay you for all of it. At least this way, I get to spread it out. Anyway, that's a month, plus an extra month's pay, because I imagine this trip will cost you a fair amount of money."

Yes, it would. For sure. And, yes, the extra month's pay would prove a lifesaver for her expenses.

Was Carl's willingness for her to go the sign from fate that she should?

"But the shows—"

"Nobody's indispensable, Cass. Yes, we'll miss you. The show will miss you. Snick and Snee will miss you. But you know what? MaryAnne was just saying that she missed the dolphins, and it would be fun to run the show for a while again. When do you want to go?"

"Well," she said, "Digger won't be back for three weeks, so after that, I guess."

"Good. I'll see about getting a student so that you can train him or her during your last week here."

It appeared to be settled. She'd work for another three weeks, using her days off to do things like getting a passport, making plane reservations, deciding what she needed to take. She'd have to inquire about all the things she needed to know, like whether to buy traveler's checks or whether her bankcard would work in Australia.

"You're very good to me, Carl. I'll do as much work as I can ahead so as to make it easier for you."

"Whatever. I'll see you tonight then." He started to go back into the house, then paused. "Listen, Cass," he said, "he looked like a fine young man. I hope things work out for you. But if they don't, you've a job here as long as you want it. You know that."

He hesitated a second time and turned to face her. "Just remember, jobs and paychecks and condos are all very well, but they don't keep you warm at night."

He walked on, into the house, to MaryAnne and the children, and closed the door behind him.

Cass sat alone in the empty office. She'd miss it. Even for a month, she'd miss the shows and the dolphins. She'd even miss the slimy frozen fish. If she never came back, she'd miss it all unbearably.

If she did come back, how could she bear Digger being out of her life forever?

Three weeks later Cass stumbled off the plane in Perth, bewildered and exhausted. Other people on the plane had spent the day and a half sleeping, but she'd been too nervous to sleep well at night, and during daylight hours, she had wanted only to gaze out the window and take in everything. It was unlikely she would ever make this trip again.

Since she'd arrived in Australia, it seemed that everything she'd seen had been red. When the plane circled Sydney airport, the impression of Sydney was of a sea of red-tile roofs, and when she flew from Sydney to Perth, the land beneath was an ocean of red earth.

When she eventually arrived in Perth, she took a

cab directly to her hotel downtown. She stumbled to her room, threw off her jogging suit—which she'd worn for comfort—and crawled into bed, where she stayed for the next sixteen hours.

When she woke up the following morning, she knew that there was no way she could drive to Dolphin Bay, guiding an unfamiliar car over unfamiliar countryside, coping with rules of the road that were opposite to those she had known, until she'd unwound and shaken off her jetlag. She was tired and hungry, and felt as if she were living in a dream.

After a late breakfast in the hotel restaurant, she began to awaken from her trance, and knew that at some point she had to acclimate herself to this new strange world. She couldn't stay in her hotel forever.

After breakfast, she wandered out into the brilliant morning sunshine. This city, full of green spaces and water, was where Digger had spent the middle third of his life, first the years of private school, then university. He had walked these streets. He had ridden these city buses. He had jogged the paths of these green parks. This was the city to which he would have brought her if she had accepted him the first time he'd proposed.

What would her life be like now, she wondered, if she had come with him then? She would have tried to transfer her courses and finish her degree here in Perth. Digger would probably have had a job teaching at the university, and she would likely have taken graduate work or teacher training. If she had come with him then, this is probably where she would now live. Instead of seeming like a dream world, this city would be home. These would be the stores she shopped in, those the parks she ran in. Driving on the left-hand side of the street would now seem the normal thing to do.

If she accepted him now, this city would not be her home. Now he would take her to a little place called Dolphin Bay, on the desolate West Coast.

Chapter Four

Cass had no problem renting a vehicle in Perth. She got a little yellow car for a very reasonable price, and was then faced with the problem of exactly what she was going to do with it. She'd learned to drive when she was a teenager, and had unrestricted use of her parents' cars until she'd left Boston.

But she had never owned a car. She still drove occasionally. A date would let her drive, or she would use Carl's car to go on an errand. In the last eight years, driving a car had become a big adventure rather than a habit. Taking this car out on the streets and driving it on the left-hand side of the road could be a very big adventure indeed.

The man who rented her the little yellow car gave her a short lesson. He didn't seem unduly concerned about the fate of his vehicle as he sat beside her, coaching her through turns in downtown Perth. She was a cautious driver and a defensive driver, looking for potential problems before they occurred, and these things helped make up for her lack of experience.

"You'll be all right," he assured her later, as he talked to her through the open window, leaning his elbows on the window ledge. "If I can give you a word of advice, though, you'd do better to stay somewhere and not travel at night. The car doesn't have 'roo bars."

" 'Roo bars? I thought you were going to warn me about all the dangers that lurk in the dark for unwary young females. What on earth are 'roo bars?"

"Kangaroos, miss. There are a lot of them up where you're going, and at night they get dazzled by the light, and often you hit them before you even know they're there. There aren't as many in the day, and you've a much better chance of seeing them. A big 'roo could make a real mess of that little car, and maybe of you too."

She understood. Just like deer in rural New England.

"All right," she assured him. "I didn't want to travel at night in a strange country anyway."

She really was in Australia, she thought with a little thrill of pleasure. The fact hadn't fully come home to her before. In many ways, Perth wasn't that different from American cities in spite of the unfamiliar dialect, and the cars on the wrong side of the road. Then, too, the sun was in the north, but she was so turned around in her directions that it looked like south, so that wasn't much different either.

The rental man shook hands with her and then drove ahead of her through the city until she was out on the main highway, which would take her first through the Darling Ranges and then on north.

She traveled for miles past orchards and wineries and farms before she began to drive through the red desert. Why couldn't Digger have had his ranch back there, she thought, rather than in the middle of this red desert, sparsely populated with cattle and sheep, the sheep dyed red from the soil around them?

The road was good, but longer than she'd imagined, and huge trucks with two or three trailers whistled by her at unthinkable speeds. Her stomach growled. She'd had nothing to eat since breakfast in the hotel. She was also beginning to understand how vast the distances were. It was fine for the drivers of the thousand and one wheelers, with their high speeds and their 'roo bars, but for an American woman who usually traveled everywhere by bus, and was too nervous to drive the speed limit, it was plain tiring.

When the highway crossed the Murchison River, she thought of following a side road a few miles, and drinking in the air of the place where Digger had grown up, but it was already four in the afternoon. She did pull to the edge of the road and stumble out of the car for a brief stretch. She could see nothing but smoke-colored shrubs and the occasional rusty sheep.

There seemed nothing to do but to put the car in gear and drive on. Her map showed a roadside motel up the highway, and she wanted to reach it in time for dinner.

She ate breakfast at the motel before she left in the morning. Most of the journey was behind her, and it was no more than another two or three hours. Now that time was upon her, she found herself procrastinating over the big sausage and egg breakfast. Traveling here was one thing, arriving quite another.

She forced herself out of the restaurant and into the car. She spent another ten minutes parked beside the road, watching a kangaroo grazing under the road sign across from the motel. It was the first one that she had seen, the warnings of the car rental man aside.

Grimly, she clenched her teeth and drove on.

When Cass arrived at Dolphin Bay, the dolphins and the tourists were there, must have been there for some time. Numbers of tourists wandered up from the beach and in and out of the tourist center. Cass parked her car and went down to the beach. Only a few diehard tourists and the ranger remained in the water.

The pelican Digger had talked about was there too, cruising up and down parallel to the shore, complete with clearly outlined bright orange beak, looking indeed, as he had in the slides, just like a bird on a paint-by-numbers picture.

And the dolphins! The water was full of them, swimming up and down. The few remaining tourists patted the dark gray sides as the animals slid by in the shallow water.

Cass approached the ranger.

"Is Digger Coady here?"

"Digger? No, no one of that—" he broke off. "Oh, you must mean Jack Coady."

"Yes," she said, "yes, his name is Jack. Digger's just a nickname."

"You're an American, aren't you? You talk like one. Is that where you met him?"

"Yes," she said, "we went to school together in Los Angeles."

"Well, that explains it then. He'd have been given the nickname there just because he's Australian. He's not known as Digger here. It's just like we might call an American here *Yank* just because he's American. You see?"

"Yes," she said. "I didn't know that then. I just know that's what everybody at UCLA called him."

"Are you a friend of Jack Coady's?"

She dodged the question. There was a tiny hollow space in the pit of her stomach. If she really meant that much to him, why hadn't he talked about her to his friends?

That wasn't really fair of her. She hadn't told anyone about him either, except Carl, and then only after Digger arrived and she asked for time off.

But if Digger hadn't told his friends about her, she wasn't about to explain. "I met him at school," she said. "We were both taking marine biology. He told me about this place, and I thought I'd like to see it. Does he still work here?"

"Oh, yes. Fine young man. Very up and coming. He's in charge here, but even at that I think he's a bit underemployed, but he loves the dolphins. In fact, he's just come back from a trip to America giving lectures and slide shows. Advertising Australia, and also trying to make people see how important it is that we start now to preserve our wildlife."

"I see," she said. The man sounded just like Digger. He seemed willing to talk about dolphins and environment and everything else. He still hadn't told her whether or not Digger was here.

She said, "Is he here now?"

He grunted. "No. He's gone into Perth on a business trip. He'll be back in a day or so."

"Oh, I see. Well, then, I'll just visit the dolphins. I work with dolphins too. I work for a small dolphinarium back in Los Angeles. I have two dolphins, and four times a week we have a show."

"Oh, yes," he said, "in America." He looked around. "Well, the last of the tourists have left. If you're familiar with dolphins, I'll just leave you here on your own. With the tourists, we have to be in the water so nobody tries to poke fingers in their blowholes, or ride on them, or feed them beer. People do the most ignorant things. However, if you work with them, you'll know better than that."

Cass bought a half-dozen fish in a bucket, kicked off her shoes, and waded into the water in her shorts.

It was a thrill to recognize the dolphins that Digger had talked about. That one, crowding close to her, had to be Bugsy. Sure enough, when she held out a fish, he snapped it up, almost taking her hand with it, and whipped around for another.

"No, you don't, my boy," she said. "I'm saving the next five for dolphins with better manners."

She could swear he scowled at her before he swam away.

There were the mother and baby, Darby and Bubbles. Cass edged closer to Darby, and held out a fish. Bugsy, ever alert, came swooping in, but Cass calmly put her body between him and Darby and fed the fish to Darby. Darby rolled over on her side as she swam past and Cass stroked her. There was a thrill from patting this beautiful wild dolphin that she just didn't get from her interaction with her own dolphins. She was very fond of Snick and Snee, but Digger was right. It wasn't quite the same.

Carefully, she tried to step around Darby so that she could pat Bubbles, but just as carefully Darby moved so that her body was always between Cass and the calf. Cass fed Darby another fish.

That must be Joan, she thought, as another adult dolphin nosed gently up to her. Joan got a fish. They were all going to get a fish—all but Bugsy. Bugsy seemed to glower at her from out in the bay. She still had two fish—one for Joan and one for Darby. Already she felt a special bond with Darby, as she stroked her side and rubbed her beak.

She was alone, except for the ranger who was busy on shore and ignored her once the last of the tourists had left. Most of the dolphins had gone also, swimming out toward deeper water. The little family of regulars still hoped that this new tourist would continue to hand over fish.

Bugsy gave up and swam out to sea, but Joan and Darby and Bubbles stayed. Joan still wanted more fish, almost as if she knew that Darby had had three to her two. Darby didn't seem to be looking for more fish. Darby seemed to be interested in friendship, in having her side stroked and her beak rubbed. Cass was happy to do this.

Finally these three, too, left, and Cass was by herself. She wandered into the visitors' center and browsed through the displays. She picked up samples of all the literature and handouts that were being given away and bought a book on the dolphins.

After she'd seen everything she wanted to at the visitors' center, Cass drove to the RV park and entered the office. Three people were there, a middle-aged woman behind the counter and a young couple chatting with her. The two latter stepped back when Cass entered.

Cass approached the counter and in response to the woman's greeting said, "I understand you rent on-site caravans here. I'd like one for about three and a half weeks."

The woman browsed through her ledger. "Sorry," she said. "Everything's booked for the next two days. After that we've a one-bedroom that would be perfect for you."

"Any place you know of that would take me for a couple days?" Digger's trailer was empty. Cass knew that, but she didn't have enough nerve to ask if she could use it until he returned.

The young woman with the mop of red curls whispered to the man with her.

"Well," the middle-aged woman said, "there is a motel in the next town. I could ring them if you liked."

The young man stepped to the counter. "Look, Miss," he said to Cass, "You're an American. I can tell by the accent. So are we. We have a three-bedroom. I think we can spare one of the rooms for a couple of nights."

She was about to refuse. Then a memory niggled at her. This must be the young couple Digger had told her about, the ones who were writers and staying at Dolphin Bay for an extended time. They were very nice, he'd said.

Besides that, she already missed Los Angeles. These were the first American voices she'd heard since she got off the plane. A wave of nostalgia hit her.

She made a token protest. "I couldn't think of imposing."

"Oh," the young woman said, "it's no imposition. It would be fun to have an American houseguest for a couple days. Not that we're homesick, but sometimes we do get a little—"

"Homesick, darlin'. That's the word you're looking for," her husband answered for her. "By the way, this is my wife, Judy. She's originally from Bangor, Maine. I'm Jon Brown and I'm from Boston. Please say you'll stay." His smile revealed a mouthful of white teeth and a sincere heart.

How could she resist? "Okay," she said. "You talked me into it. I grew up in Boston too." She shook hands with both Judy and Jon. "I'm Cass Chase. I work with dolphins in Los Angeles, and I'm very pleased to meet you."

"Let's go right now," Judy said. Cass liked Judy. She seemed a true extrovert, bubbling over with friendship and enthusiasm.

Judy added, "We'll have coffee. Want coffee?"

Did she want coffee? Do dolphins want fish? It seemed that she hadn't had a cup of really good coffee since she'd left Los Angeles.

"Love it."

"Let's go. It's down this path, then to your left."

Cass looked sideways at Jon and Judy as they walked three abreast, Judy in the middle. Digger had been right. They were a very good-looking couple. Judy appeared to be a mass of freckles, and she wore no makeup. Still, she seemed an extremely attractive woman with her slender figure, cap of red curls, green-gray eyes, and golden eyebrows and lashes. Jon towered above them both. His curls, shorter than Judy's, were black, his eyes a piercing blue.

He didn't look like a Harvard professor. He looked like a real hunk—almost as handsome as Digger.

Cass looked around her. Tidy rows of caravans—what she'd have called mobile homes—were set in neat streets with narrow roads between them. Some had flowers around them. Others, the ones for short-term stays, she supposed, had only earth out front, covered by white shells. All were white, looking freshly painted with trim of various colors.

They reached the caravan belonging to Jon and Judy. It was spacious, almost like a small bungalow. Cass sat down at the kitchen table across from Judy while Jon made coffee. The interior of the caravan was as tidy as the outside, Cass noticed. Off-white vinyl flooring covered the kitchen floor, and the counters were a cheery bright blue, which reflected the accents on the lamps and curtains.

Cass turned around and looked into the living room. "The pictures on the walls are very different," she said. "What are they?"

"Oh," Judy said. "They're enlarged and framed book covers. Jon's a writer."

"We're both writers, darlin'," Jon said, then turned to Cass. "We both have framed covers on those walls. I'll show them to you when we've finished our coffee. We also have three bedrooms and two bathrooms. You can have a grand tour of the whole place."

"I'd love a tour," Cass said. "For now, tell me about yourselves. How did you meet?"

"Well," John said, "we were both traveling in New Zealand."

"Met in New Zealand?" Cass had known that already from Digger, but she feigned ignorance for the sake of the story. "Tell me all about it."

Judy giggled. "You won't believe this, but my dad hired Jon to keep an eye on me. Anonymously of course. Well, not really hired, because they were friends. It was a freebie. I was livid when I found out. So Jon threw me across his saddle and took me to a lawyer in Christchurch where he posted a fifty thousand-dollar bond that he had good intentions. That didn't leave me any less livid, I'll tell you."

Cass thought of her own relationship with Digger. "You must have forgiven him. The whole thing sounds awfully romantic."

Judy giggled again. She had a charming giggle, lively without sounding silly. "Oh, yes," she said. "Frightfully. Who can resist a man if he writes a song for you and sings it all over New Zealand?"

Cass sighed. "You seem awfully in love," she said.

"Yes," Judy said. "He is my life. And I am his."

They fell silent. Jon appeared with three cups of coffee. Cass inhaled the steam rising from her mug.

"Heaven," she said. "Just heaven."

"I'll show you your room in a few minutes," Jon said, "and let you unpack. We have two spare rooms, a study for each of us."

"You'll have mine," Judy said. "Just give me a chance to unplug my laptop. I'll move it into Jon's study for the next couple of days. That way you can sleep in as long as you like. You see, our schedule is writing from eight to twelve every morning. Then we spend the rest of the day as we wish. Jon puts coffee on at seven. You can either join us for breakfast then or forage for yourself later. For now, do whatever you want. We'll have dinner at six. They call it *tea* here."

Cass reflected. *He is my life,* Judy had said. Cass had operated on the premise that her career and her apartment were her life. It would be very nice if she could fit Digger into them. Maybe that wasn't the way it worked. Jon and Judy apparently wandered the earth like a pair of gypsies, needing only each other. However, unlike Judy, Cass couldn't fit her career into a laptop computer.

She'd think about all of it later.

Digger had been right about one thing—she needed this time to examine him in his own habitat, as her professors at UCLA would have put it.

She was glad she'd come.

* * *

Dinner was simple—barbecued steak, baked potatoes, and a green salad. Jon and Judy prepared it together.

"I'm afraid I'm not much of a cook," Judy said. "When I lived at home, my mother did that. Later, when I was teaching I sort of survived on fast food and frozen TV dinners. Jon's been teaching me. But I do make a mean Pavlova. I learned that one on my own to impress him when we first met."

"Pavlova?"

"Yes. It's sort of the national dessert of New Zealand and Australia. Both of them claim to have invented it. It's really just whipped egg whites, loaded with sugar. Then you bake it and fill it with fruit and whipped cream." She looked dreamy. "To die for."

After the meal was finished and the dishes done, Cass wandered outside on her own to breathe in the night air and look at the stars.

The stars were different here. The familiar constellations were missing, replaced by new and unknown ones.

Cass squinted as she looked into the heavens. Somewhere up there was the fabled Southern Cross. There were two possibilities, two crosses in the Australian sky. She started back to the trailer to ask Jon and Judy, then hesitated.

Digger was coming in a day or two. She'd explored Los Angeles with Digger.

She wanted to explore West Australia with him too. She'd wait for him to show her the Southern Cross.

The next night, when dinner was over, Jon picked up his guitar and they all made their way to the center of the campground area where a bonfire already blazed. A group of people, most of them young, sat on logs of driftwood arranged in a circle around the fire.

There were rounds of greetings. Cass was introduced to each person in the group. She'd never remember. She knew that. The others probably would, because she was the new kid on the block.

People moved over to make room for Jon and Judy and Cass to sit together.

This seemed to be, if not a nightly ritual, at least a common one.

Jon tuned his guitar, strummed a few chords, and the campfire group began with several rousing stanzas of "Waltzing Matilda." They then drifted into other Australian folk songs, then, as this was a mixed group of many nationalities, into folk songs of many countries. Jon seemed to know them all, or at least be able to chord along once someone had hummed the tune.

There was a pause in the singing. Jon cleared his throat, plunked out an unfamiliar melody for a few notes, looked at Judy and began to sing.

I wooed you in Auckland, I wed you in Christchurch,

Wilma Fasano

I chased you all over the New Zealand Coast.
When we were married, we went to Australia.
And it's at Dolphin Bay, that I love you the most.

There were more stanzas, but Cass wasn't capable of listening any longer.

Judy and Jon had entered a world of their own, a world where only the two of them existed.

A sudden burst of tears stung Cass's eyes, and round wet drops rolled down her cheeks. The love between Jon and Judy pulsed and vibrated, a shining living thing. It was so beautiful Cass couldn't bear it.

She thought about herself and Digger. Could they ever capture a love like this instead of the present situation? *We have to get acquainted again. I can't leave my job. I can't leave Australia!* Had Jon and Judy gone through all these questions and doubts?

"Excuse me," Cass murmured to Judy. "I'm going back for a moment to the washroom." She turned and fled down the path that led to the mobile, her vision fixated on the trail beneath her feet because of things she'd heard about snakes in Australia. The bushes on either side darkened the path.

She hustled around a corner. Something large and hard hit her. The breath escaped her lungs with a swoosh, and she landed on her backside. From out of the dark, a hand grasped hers and hauled her to her feet.

She gasped. "Digger!" At the same time, he gasped and said, "Cass!"

They paused to catch their breath.

"What are you doing here?"

"You invited me if you remember?"

"Yes. I didn't think you'd come." His voice was filled with a tenderness that almost reminded her of Jon and Judy. "You came. Cass, you came."

"Yes," she said. Now she was here, now he was here, she couldn't think of another thing to say, so she said the first thing that came into her head. "I want you to show me the Southern Cross."

He chuckled then, and drew her against him. He bent down so he could rest his cheek against hers, and rocked her in his arms. "Oh, Cass," he murmured, "it's so good to see you." He released her, but continued to hold her hand snug in his.

"Come on, lady," he said. "Let's go down to the beach and I'll show you the Southern Cross."

They walked, hand in hand, to the beach, across the beach, and out on the long jetty that split the bay. His hand was warm and comforting. For that moment, home was neither Los Angeles nor Australia, but simply wherever Digger was.

He stepped back so that he stood behind her and wrapped one arm around her, his hand still holding hers. Then he maneuvered both of them to face the direction he wanted.

"All right, Cass," he said. "We're facing south now."

Could have fooled her. It seemed like north to her,

always had, always would. South was where the sun and moon lived, and south was to her back. She knew that was wrong, but she also knew that, for her, it would never change.

He pointed ahead with their clasped hands. "Now," he said, "you see that group of bright stars in the form of a cross? Sailors used it to navigate by, the same as sailors in North America used the Big Dipper and the North Star."

"But," she said, "I looked earlier for it, by myself. And there are two of them."

"Yes," he said, and told her which was the right one. "The other one is commonly called the False Cross. Okay. You've got the right one now?"

"Yes," she said.

He kissed the top of her head. "Tell you what," he said. "Why don't we just sit on the jetty and neck?"

"That's an old-fashioned word," she said.

"I know. What I have in mind is old-fashioned rec-reation. I don't want to do any of those things the modern terms suggest. I just want to neck."

He drew her down with him to sit on the jetty. "Come on now," he said. "I'll sit cross-legged here, and you snuggle back against me. We'll stare at the Southern Cross, and I'll occasionally plant a kiss on the nape of your neck. Agreed?"

"Agreed." She pivoted around so that her back was to him, then inched her way backward until they were snuggled up together. He placed both arms loosely around her. "Good," he said. "Bonzer, in fact. My sheila. You'll have to remember all this Australian lingo, you know."

She wasn't sure whether she'd have to do that or not, but she sure wasn't going to rock the boat by arguing about it now.

"So where are you staying?" He blew on her neck until her hair parted, then planted a kiss on the nape as he'd promised. A shiver of delight passed through her.

"With Jon and Judy Brown for last night and to-night. Then I'm getting a camper-van of my own. A one-bedroom." She paused. "You were right," she said. "Jon and Judy are really nice."

"You know who he is?"

"What do you mean, who he is? He's a writer. So's she."

"Yeah, he's a writer all right. He's Jonathon Marlowe."

"The best-selling novelist? The one who writes adventure novels that make your hair stand straight up on end?"

"The very one. His full name is Jonathon Marlowe Brown."

"Oh." She hadn't realized that her impromptu host was famous.

"You still see the Southern Cross?"

"Yes. Beautiful, isn't it? Can't you just imagine all

those early sailors who looked to it to find their way home?"

His lips touched the side of her neck.

"That's nice," she said.

"Yeah. Maybe that's why it's called necking."

They sat in silence. Cass breathed deeply. She could stay here forever, peaceful and quiet with Digger's arms around her. It was a moment to treasure out of the turbulence of their past relationship.

Chapter Five

As she sat on the jetty with Digger, Cass's eyes adjusted to the dark. The buildings and boats around her became more than darker shapes in a dark night.

"What are the boats on that side of the jetty?" She pointed to the side of the bay across the pier from where the dolphins came.

"Fishing boats. Private yachts. A mixed bag." He pointed to an old fishing boat, the one farthest up the jetty. "See that one? We're concerned about that one. Nobody knows what he's up to. Selling drugs? Stealing dolphins? We don't know. If any of us approach him, he knows who we are, and everything's very innocent. He's not here all the time. He comes and goes. If he's fishing, it's sure not obvious. He's occasionally away for days at a time. Drugs? He looks the type, but not likely. This isn't exactly Sydney or Melbourne. He wouldn't have enough market here to pay for his gas."

"So what do you think?"

"I'm afraid it's the dolphins. That he's tracking the dolphins and when he's out of sight of the bay where one of us would see him, he captures them and takes them and sells them for zoos or marine shows—things of that nature. But we can't prove it. If he does it, the action all takes place far enough out to sea that we couldn't do anything about it anyway. None of the dolphins we recognize and have named are missing. But others come in occasionally. It's impossible to tell."

"What's he like?"

"Scruffy. Like an old-time hippie who's old enough to retire, but thinks he's still young and it's still the 1960s. He's known simply as Jenkins. Last name? First name? Nickname? Nobody knows. All we know is that he spends a lot of time tied up to this jetty and when he leaves, nobody knows where he goes. Enough about that. Let's talk about you. Like how long you're staying."

"A month altogether. But some of that's already gone, and there's still the travel time going home."

"Mmm. A bit over three weeks then. That's wonderful. And you're spending all of it here?"

"I'd like to," she said.

"And I'd like you to."

Yes, she'd spend the whole time here. Unless, of course, Digger and she decided to part ways first. Then there'd be no point. That would not be likely. There was a tacit agreement that they wouldn't talk about anything that mattered until a few days before she left, so there'd be nothing to quarrel about. Until then she was a tourist with a little light-hearted summer romance thrown in. Or was this winter?

Digger rubbed his cheek against hers. His emerging beard, unshaven since the morning, rubbed her face.

She wished she could be more to him than a summer romance. She wished she could do something for him, something important, a grand gesture.

She thought of the derelict fishing boat owned by the man called Jenkins, the one Digger suspected of catching dolphins. Nobody could get near him, Digger had said, because he knew they were watching him.

But what about her? To the man Jenkins, she was just another tourist. Could she strike up a friendship, drink coffee with him, ask leading questions? Apparently he had no friends. Would he relax his guard to someone who extended the hand of friendship?

She started to speak, then stopped. No. If she mentioned this to Digger, he'd forbid her to get involved. He wouldn't understand that there was no real danger. She wouldn't go further than the outside deck where she was in public view. If she suspected Jenkins might harm her, she'd forget the whole thing.

It was something she'd think through a little more clearly before she made any decisions.

Would it be unethical of her to pretend to be friends so she could catch him in wrongdoing? Not really. If he were stealing dolphins, he deserved to be tricked. If he weren't, he'd never know that she was anything but a friendly tourist.

"Come on," Digger said. "Time to turn in. I have to work tomorrow. I'll walk you back."

They walked through the velvet night, hand in hand. At the door to Jon's trailer, he took her in his arms and kissed her. His lips were warm and firm against her own.

"See you tomorrow, Cass," he said. "I'll book off an extra hour and take you for lunch. Pick you up here at twelve."

Lunch would be nice, but not nearly as nice as tonight. Lunch would not include a velvet night sky nor firm, warm lips.

Digger made his way slowly back to his own trailer.

So, she'd come to him after all, his golden girl from California. Did that mean that she still cared? Cared enough to marry him maybe? He'd have to stop living with his dreams of times past and decide whether he still wanted to marry her. He'd made no promises, simply said that they must get to know each other again.

But her coming this far was a promise in itself.

He entered his trailer. It was neat and tidy. He'd washed the floor and stacked the dishes in the dishwasher. But something was missing. It was a bachelor pad. It didn't have the woman's touch.

He thought of her condo in Los Angeles. The red dishes, the navy tablecloth, the candles that were just right.

A wave of longing hit him. Longing to have this woman forever, to love and cherish her. To between them make their home a warm and loving place.

He'd see. He had two people to convince—Cass and himself.

After Digger had kissed Cass goodnight and she'd disappeared into the mobile, she puttered around the small room that was Judy's study. The last few days had gone by in a haze. In some ways, what she was doing right now seemed like a dream, and soon she would wake up and find herself back in the apartment in Los Angeles. At other times, it seemed that the life in Los Angeles was so far away that it appeared to be the dream, and this was the life she had always lived.

She brushed her teeth, put on the oversized T-shirt she slept in, propped herself up on her pillows, turned on the bedside light and began to read the literature she'd picked up at the tourist center, but soon she had drifted back to thoughts of Digger.

Jack, she reminded herself. Here, she'd have to speak of him as Jack. She couldn't think of him as

Jack. Jack was such an ordinary name; there was certainly nothing ordinary about Digger. He'd always be Digger to her, but, except when they were alone, she'd really have to start calling him Jack.

Thoughts of him had been chasing each other around in her mind, like squirrels in a cage, ever since they'd parted in Los Angeles. How did she feel about him? Did she love him? Could they ever have the kind of love that throbbed palpably between Jon and Judy? Would they marry? It was hard to imagine being married to anyone but Digger, but when she thought about it, it was pretty hard to imagine being married to Digger too.

If things appeared to go in that direction, could she give up her job, her home, the security she had worked for, and gamble on the love of one man in a strange world? The world suited her. No doubt about that. The dolphins. The space. The beauty of the green ocean and the blue skies and the red earth all around her.

It was an Eden, into which the serpent had already intruded in the shape of a man named Jenkins.

Cass's mind turned to the old fishing boat and the man who might harm the dolphins she had come to know and love. She knew that there was already a bond growing between herself and Darby.

If she struck up a friendship with Jenkins and Digger found out, it might well be the end of their relationship. But if she took the easy way out and ignored the situation, and Jenkins took away Darby and Bubbles, she would never be able to forgive herself.

As the questions and thoughts and doubts revolved in her mind, she totally forgot the book she'd started to read.

Gradually it fell from her hand and she drifted off to sleep. She dreamed that a dolphin dressed up in a tuxedo was making her do tricks. He stood up on the side of the pool, and she was in the water. When he waved his stick, she performed.

She was dressed in her red sequined performing costume. When the dolphin moved his baton, she had to leap up high out of the water and jump through hoops.

He threw her a raw fish as a reward, and just as she was starting to eat it, she realized the dolphin was really Darby, and Darby was saying, *Look what happened to me because you let him take me.*

Cass woke up to find herself chewing on the end of the pillow. She sat up, shaking all over, and ran her hands through her hair, trying to rid herself of the troublesome dream.

Promptly at twelve noon the next day, Digger appeared at the door, driving a rugged four-wheel-drive sports utility vehicle. He took Cass to the closest small town where they ate at a restaurant made of shells.

Digger told her that the restaurant, as well as several other buildings in town, was built of shells from a local beach. The shells were piled so deep on the beach that they compressed, and were quarried like stone. When they stopped at the front to pay the bill, the waitress advised Cass to see the beach, and Digger said that, yes, he'd take the young lady there right away.

The beach appeared to stretch forever, at a distance looking like white sand. Digger parked his truck at the end of a red sand road. The two of them walked to the beach, holding hands and swinging them as children do. The beach was made up of millions of small white shells. It extended a considerable distance back from the water and along the shore as far as they could see.

Digger gave Cass the tour-guide information on the shells. They were discarded regularly by small sea organisms and went to depths of thirty feet or more. The bottom levels were compacted with the weight of the upper ones, creating solid blocks that were quarried and used for building.

"I don't see any quarries," Cass said. "Why not?"

Digger shrugged. "Don't know," he said. "Maybe the digging is down the beach out of sight. Or maybe they don't do it anymore. I've only been up here a few years. I'll ask somebody and find out for you."

"Doesn't really matter. The important thing is that the water's blue and the beach is white, and it looks like a great place to sit and ponder infinity. Or something."

Cass dropped to the beach and pulled Digger down beside her. They both sat with their knees up, arms wrapped around their knees, and stared without speaking into the azure waters of the bay.

What was Digger thinking of? Was he also pondering their future?

When it came time for her to leave, would he propose? If he did, what would she say? Marrying Digger would mean the end of any career for her.

It wouldn't be any use to try to get Digger to move. She'd already tried that. Now that she'd been here, she couldn't blame him. Who would trade this beautiful state of West Australia and its dolphins, for the freeways and ghettos of a city?

But how could she get a job? She'd probably have to get some sort of work permit from the government, and she had no experience in that sort of thing. The only thing she knew about governments was that they moved very slowly and that there was always a lot of red tape.

Then, any available job would probably be in Perth. Perth was still too far away from Dolphin Bay to run a marriage successfully. She could apply for a job as a ranger at Dolphin Bay, but she'd have very little chance of getting it. The ranger she'd met the first day had told her that Digger was in charge here. If she married Digger, and she wouldn't be applying for jobs if she didn't, he would never hire her, not unless there was nobody else available—unlikely. He was far too honorable and would consider it nepotism.

The only possible jobs available for her here would be ones as a waitress or housekeeper or saleslady in a souvenir shop. Local people would probably have first chance at those, and, if not, they were likely seasonal, and there was a limit to what degree she was willing to be underemployed.

Dolphin research would be interesting, but she had no idea whether the Australian government or universities had grants for this. She did know that it would take far too long to find out. No, if she married Digger, she would have to reconcile herself to being the little housewife waiting for him to come home from work every day. She didn't want to give up a life of her own to that degree.

Forget all this, she told herself. For the next three weeks, she'd be an American woman on vacation. If she could help Digger prevent Jenkins from stealing the dolphins, all to the good.

Digger placed his hand on her back and scratched gently at her sweater with the tips of his fingers. She purred. His hand felt very much like a nice back-scratcher in the shower.

"Come on," he said. "You've pondered infinity long enough. Let's get on to the *or something*."

He stopped scratching her back, and instead cupped her head and forced her to face him. He lowered his mouth to hers. She sighed and then let herself free to drown in the pleasure of his soft kisses, in the warmth of his hand on her head, in the distinctly enjoyable feelings that were the result of all this.

When the kisses ceased, she rested her temple against the side of his neck and felt the throbbing of his veins.

"Oh, Digger," she murmured.

He rocked her for a moment, then released her and stood up. He held out his hand.

"Time to go," he said. "I'm a working man."

Reluctantly, she grasped his hand and levered herself up from the beach. She brushed off the clinging shells. Her skin was imprinted with the shapes all the way up her legs and even through her denim shorts.

Much as Dolphin Bay had already imprinted itself on her.

When Cass and Digger got back from the shell beach, Digger went directly to his office and booted up the computer. He'd fallen behind on his bookwork when he was away. Now with Cass here, he'd lose even more time. Not that he'd have it any other way. He wanted to show her this niche of country that he loved. He hoped that he could convince her to love it too.

He worked away on budgets and inventory and all the other rare and exciting things that business offices produce. When he couldn't stand it anymore, he went to the window and stretched, placing his palms on the small of his back to ease out the cramped muscles that deskwork creates.

He looked out. The dolphins had appeared and with them a horde of tourists and a couple of rangers. He scanned the crowd to find Cass. She came to the beach while he watched.

She fascinated him. Even the act of buying a bucket of fish looked glamorous when Cass did it. After she bought the fish, she kicked off her beach sandals and waded in. She looked like a sheep dog, cutting out the ones she wanted—not surprisingly, Bugsy, Joan, and Darby with her baby. Other dolphins circled Cass hoping for fish, but she ignored them.

Digger continued watching. The computer could wait.

Each of her three got two fish. Then when the fish were gone, she stroked their sides, and as they got more comfortable with her, she scratched their beaks. Even Bugsy let his side be stroked a couple of times, but when she moved her hand up to his beak, he sidled away. Cass probably didn't know that, but the regular tourists weren't permitted to as much as touch him.

There was no doubt—Cass had a real feeling for the dolphins. Digger was glad. He'd been a little dubious about her trained animal act back in Los Angeles, and was relieved to see her real affinity with the dolphins here. He still wanted to marry her, but had become more levelheaded than he'd been six years ago. No matter how much he loved her, any marriage built on nothing but attraction would be doomed to failure. It was reassuring that, in spite of her big-city background, she treasured the land, the sea, and the dolphins.

A couple of times, she tried to pat little Bubbles, but Darby, although she herself had become very friendly with Cass, still kept herself firmly between Cass and the baby. She didn't appear to be angry with Cass for trying, but somehow she was always there, swimming in between, so that all Cass's attempts ended in failure.

It was a beautiful tableau, but Digger, much as he wanted to, couldn't stand here and watch all afternoon.

Reluctantly, he turned back to his computer.

That night, Cass sat alone on the beach looking at the stars and breathing in the evening air. The tourists had all returned to the campground or were back on their tour buses, starting the return journey down the long road to Perth. The rangers had gone home to their trailers in the campground, or to their houses in the area. Digger was working in the office. They'd go for a moonlit walk before bedtime, he'd promised her. Everything was dead quiet. The moon, riding peacefully in the northern sky, reflected on the waters of the bay.

Cass wore shorts, and a heavy sweater over her tank top. The sweater protected her from the cool night air. She sat, knees drawn up, and arms wrapped around them. Her chin rested on her knees, and she gazed at the moon and at the Southern Cross.

Then she saw them far out in the bay, the dolphins cavorting in the water, moonlight gleaming on their sleek, dark backs. The few regulars came nosing in to the beach. Cass shed her sweater.

"Sorry, girls, no fish tonight," she said as she waded in. "The fish store's closed." Darby came up anyway, happy to have her beak scratched.

Cass backed away and clapped her hands and whistled to Darby. The dolphin, curious, swam up to her. Cass rewarded her with patting and scratching, then moved a little further away and clapped and whistled again.

Darby enjoyed the game. What a joy she was. Then Joan came up, also responding to the game and being scratched and patted. Although there were no food rewards, the dolphins seemed to enjoy the sport for itself. Only Bugsy stayed apart, aloof and suspicious, seeming to say, *There's no fish tonight. Why should I bother?*

The playing went on for two hours before the dolphins tired and went back to sea.

Cass looked down at her legs. Her shorts were soaked. Digger still hadn't appeared. She moved on up to the visitor's center, entered and tapped on Digger's office door.

Digger looked up as Cass entered. "Oh, hi," he said. "Sorry about that. I had good intentions. Got busy with all this work." He started to shuffle papers and put them into folders. "Be with you in a moment. Still want to go for a walk?"

She looked down at her sopping shorts. "Not without changing, I guess," she said. "The dolphins came in tonight. They played with me in the water for a couple hours, Darby and Joan. And Bugsy, sort of. Bugsy doesn't really play, but he was there." She swallowed. "It was magic," she said. "The night, the moon, the Southern Cross, the dolphins. I know why you love it."

"Yes," he said, as he stood up, put his arms around her, and held her, ignoring her dampness. "I thought if only you'd come, you'd understand."

Yes, she understood. She waited while he locked up, then silently put her hand into his. She understood. But she also understood that there was nothing here for her. Playing with dolphins and doing gourmet cooking for two people didn't add up to a fulfilling career.

She looked up the jetty. The old boat belonging to the man they called Jenkins was there. Tomorrow morning, when she was sure that Jon and Judy were writing, and Digger was immersed in his bookwork, she'd put her plan into operation. At least, before she left, she could do something for the dolphins and for Digger.

* * *

In the morning, once she was sure that Digger was busy in his office, Cass wandered up the long jetty toward the place where Jenkins' old boat was tied. She'd heard more about the man, not just from Digger, but from comments by other rangers and some remarks from Jon and Judy. The consensus of opinion was that he was a loner, not interested in passing the time chatting with the locals. She'd discovered that he was long-haired, bearded, and dirty, and not as young as he tried to pretend. From the description, she knew she wouldn't have wanted to meet him in a back alley, but surely he couldn't harm her in the middle of the morning with other people and fishing boats all around.

His aloofness made him disliked among the locals and the rangers. Everybody knew about the other boats on the jetty, the vacationers and the fishermen, and chatted freely with their owners. The suspicion was that Jenkins's boat peddled drugs and that when it made its excursions out of port that it was probably making exchanges with other boats. Cass thought Digger's theory about the dolphins was more likely, but she hadn't heard that one anywhere else.

She sauntered along slowly, stopping to greet tourists on the jetty or in the water. As the water deepened and the only people were on boats tied to the jetty, she said "Good Morning" to everyone she saw. If the rangers or Digger noticed her, all she was doing was ambling along, speaking to everyone.

When she reached Jenkins' boat and saw the man out on the open deck, her first close-up view of him, she realized that Digger was right. Close up and behind the beard, he was older than he appeared at a distance. His blond beard and hair were streaked with gray, and there were lines around his eyes. He looked twenty years out of date.

He wore a muscle shirt with torn jeans. On his feet were leather sandals. The feet in them apparently had never seen water, soapy, salt, or otherwise. He appeared to be one of the sixties hippies who had never grown up.

Well, that wasn't her concern. If she could find out what he was up to, that was all that mattered.

He was out on deck, lounging in a chair and smoking. He saw her and looked up. A shiver passed through her spine. He looked as if he'd like to get his hands on her, but when she stopped to think about it, that didn't much concern her. She'd been taking care of herself in this respect all her adult life. She could run fast and had done very well in several courses in self-defense. She could also swim fast if she had to.

"Hi," she said.

He got to his feet. "Hi, there, beautiful. I've seen you around. Could I interest you in a drink?"

She shook her head, deliberately looking much more stupid and naive than she was.

"Sorry," she called to him. "I don't drink. Do you have coffee?"

"Sure thing." He held out a grimy nicotine-stained hand, and helped her jump across from the jetty to the deck.

Against her instincts and desires, she left her hand in his and introduced herself. "I'm Cass Chase from Los Angeles. Just here for a short time as a tourist."

He shook her hand. "Hi. I'm Tim Jenkins. I usually just go by Jenkins. Pleased to meet you. I'll have to get the coffee ready. Do you want to come forward? It's really nice there."

"No," she said. "I get seasick when I'm closed in." She removed her hand from his and resisted the temptation to wipe it on her shorts.

He looked across the flat expanse of Dolphin Bay on a windless morning. "Yeah, right," he said. "I'm sure you do."

She chucked the stupid and naive image. There really wasn't much point to it anyway. "Well, I say I do. You can believe what you want. Now, do I get coffee or not?"

He sighed with resignation. "I suppose so. Now why don't you just sit yourself down in this chair while I get it ready?"

Trying to keep her reluctance from being obvious, she took the chair he'd just vacated, determining to wash her clothes the minute she got back to the campground. As soon as he disappeared forward, she wiped her hand on her shorts.

She looked casually at the boat. Aft, where she sat,

was an open space. At the moment, it held a number of deck chairs folded up along the edge. She sat in the only unfolded chair. A low railing protected the unwary from falling overboard.

The forward area, closed in, undoubtedly held the galley, the bunks, and the controls. She noted that the boat did appear to have the appropriate paraphernalia for fishing—bought with the boat, she presumed, and kept for stage dressing. She noted a large plastic swimming pool at the front of the deck. There were also nets and a variety of ropes. A sort of portable gangplank was propped against the railing. That would be used for getting back and forth to small boats. All of this supported Digger's theory. A dolphin could be kept in the swimming pool for a short period of time and tied down with the ropes to eliminate any risk of its jumping out.

Jenkins came with the coffee and sat on the floor near Cass's feet, facing her. The top of his head was as dirty as his feet. She shuddered a bit. The boat itself was cleaner than she would have expected.

She took the coffee and sipped it warily. It was surprisingly good and the cup appeared to be clean. She drank the rest slowly, but with pleasure, as they talked.

"So," she said, "nice boat."

"Thanks. I like it."

"You're a fisherman, are you?"

"Depends on your definition of fishing, I guess. I

make my living from the sea, yes." He leered at her. "And what do you do?"

"Actually," she said, "I run a dolphin show. A small one in Los Angeles."

"That's interesting. It's successful?"

"Sort of." She shrugged. It seemed the conversation might go very well if she steered it the right way. "It would be a lot more successful if we had more dolphins. We have just two. They're getting old, and if we can't replace them, that will be the end of the show."

His eyes were slitted against the sun, and this gave him a somewhat sinister appearance when he looked at her.

"It would sure be nice if we could find more dolphins. Especially ones that would be easy to work with and train," she said.

"That's expensive, you know."

"I'm sure it would be. The ones we have now were free. They'd been caught in a fisherman's net, and he gave them to my boss."

"Yeah. Not many people give things away."

"I know. We couldn't be lucky enough for that to happen again. I guess I'll just have to find another job."

"I might be able to help you out with the dolphins, but first I have to be sure that, whether we do business or not, you'll keep this private."

"I guess I know when to keep my mouth shut. Why?"

"Well, that's what I do, sort of. I sell dolphins. How you'd get them to Los Angeles would be your problem."

She felt trapped. The last thing in the world she wanted was to be responsible for his taking more dolphins. She back-pedaled.

"Hmm," she said. "Well, I'm not really authorized to make bargains. My boss is in charge of that sort of thing. I'd have to see what he thought."

"Hey," he said. "You do that. If your boss wants to do business, come talk to me again."

"Well," she said, "I'll talk to him, but I'm not sure. He really loves animals. He got these as sort of a rescue operation, but I don't know whether he'd go along with buying wild ones. You see, a lot of people think it's wrong to capture animals for display."

"Hey," he said. "What's wrong with that? The sharks eat them. They get captured in fishermen's nets and drown. Which would you prefer? To be drowned and eaten by sharks, or to have a nice home where you're well treated and have lots to eat without working for it? Hey, no problem."

"I'd rather have the good home," she agreed.

He spread his hands out, palms up. "Well, that's up to you, isn't it? You're the one who brought this up and said you needed more dolphins. If you want to talk to him and see what he's willing to pay, you just do that. You want to do business, come see me again. If you just want to drop by for coffee, come see me again anyway."

Clearly, she'd been dismissed for now. She stood up.

"Good-bye," she said formally.

He held up his fingers in the '60s gesture. "Peace," he said.

Chapter Six

After her visit to Jenkins, Cass ambled back down the jetty at the same pace as she'd come up, stopping to chat with everyone along the way. When she got back, the dolphins, the tourists, and one ranger were in the water. Digger must be in the office, doing his everlasting bookwork.

She brought her hand up to her head to tidy her hair. She might as well trot in and chat with him too. With a bit of luck he'd be free for lunch. She'd offer to make him a sandwich.

She was nervous about seeing him, afraid that somehow he'd become aware of her visit to Jenkins. Not that he'd be jealous. The idea of someone who looked like Digger being jealous of someone who looked like Jenkins was downright laughable. However, he wouldn't approve. She knew that for sure. He'd probably worry about her too and lecture her on the risks of fraternizing with the dregs of society. She daren't tell him what she'd been up to or he'd never let her out of his sight again.

Not that that would be all bad.

However, she must see him and get it over with. She'd know from the first look whether he knew or not.

She tapped on the door.

"It's open."

She walked in.

"Hi," he said. "Coffee? I've got some on. Picked up that habit in Los Angeles."

"Sure." If she drank any more coffee, she wouldn't sleep for three weeks, but she wasn't about to tell him that.

He got up and poured out two mugs of coffee from the percolator that sat on the filing cabinet.

"Here," he said, as he shoved the mug across the desk. "Now, why don't you sit down." He waved toward the chair in front of his desk, and sat down himself, behind his desk.

"So, what've you been up to? Sorry I've been too busy to spend much time with you."

He didn't know. That much was obvious. However, she'd better tell him most of the truth, just in case.

"I walked around," she said. "Talked to people. I walked to the end of the jetty and back. It's really long. Then I watched the tourists watching the dolphins. Then I came here to see if you're free for lunch. I'll feed you," she added.

"Let me just take a look down the beach and see if everything's in order there." He moved to the window, and stood, looking out, with his hands resting on the bottom sill.

Impulsively she went to him, encircled his waist with her arms, and laid her cheek against his back. She could feel the muscles of his stomach quiver where she touched them.

He lifted one hand to check his watch.

"All right," he said. "I'll meet you in half an hour."

She squeezed him and nipped his back lightly with her teeth through his cotton shirt, then once more rested her cheek against his back.

"I'll be down at the beach," she said and slipped out quietly.

She sat on the sand, waiting for Digger to finish his office work and join her. What would she say if he wanted to marry her? What would she do if he didn't?

She sighed. There was no point sitting here and thinking herself into a major depression. She looked at the water. Most of the dolphins had left. All of the tourists had left. The fish booth was closed. Darby and Joan and Bubbles still lingered.

She stood up, kicked off her shoes, and waded into the water.

Darby saw her and eased through the water on her side, one eye pointing up, the other under water.

I wonder what they see that way? Cass thought. *What is your view of the world when one eye is under water and the other in the air?*

Darby nosed up to her.

Cass scratched her absently. "Sorry, old girl," she said. "No fish today."

Darby didn't seem to care. She rubbed against Cass, almost like a domestic cat.

She was so good, so trusting. Cass was plunged into depression at the thought that someday Jenkins might capture her in his nets and bear her away to captivity.

Darby appeared to be puzzled by the strange behavior of her favorite human. She touched Cass with her beak, and brushed against her legs again, but Cass's caresses had no warmth in them. Darby swam a short distance away, and then Cass realized what she was doing. She was nosing little Bubbles toward Cass, so that Cass could pet her.

This was the first time Cass had been able to get near Bubbles. She suspected that no human but Digger had ever touched Bubbles, and she knew that any of the other people around would have felt a deep feeling of peace from this gesture of trust.

She patted Bubbles, and felt even worse. Jenkins might capture her too, or worst of all he might capture Darby and leave Bubbles to starve.

How could she get proof about Jenkins that would

stand up in court and, once and for all, remove the threat he posed to the dolphins?

She sank down and sat in the water. Darby came over and placed her head in Cass's lap while little Bubbles hovered nearby, not realizing what was going on, but enjoying the preoccupied pats and scratchings which she had never before been permitted to share.

Cass rubbed Darby's beak until her thoughts blanked out and her senses went numb and, in spite of all, a sort of peace stole over her.

They were like that when Digger came down to the beach, still wearing the brown shirt and shorts that were his uniform. Cass's eyes were at knee level. The sun-bleached hairs of his legs glistened in the morning light.

He walked into the water and leaned over so as to give Darby a few scratches. She raised her head from Cass's lap and squeaked with joy at seeing him again. She swam around and came to him, circling around his legs.

"Hi, old girl," he said to her. "Has your baby been playing with any tin cans lately? Doesn't look like it, does it?" he added as he gave the baby's beak a glance. "A real little beauty you've got yourself there, Darby!"

He left Darby and hauled Cass to her feet, looking at her critically.

"Hey," he said, "next time you want to sit around in the water, why don't you wear your swim togs?

Come on. Get out of the water and up to your caravan and change. You promised me lunch. Remember? Have a fast shower and I'll turn up in another fifteen minutes or so."

He reached out and took her hand to lead her up to the beach. He slapped her wet bottom. "Come on, Cass. Run. I know it's warm, but it's still time for you to move."

Dutifully she began jogging across the beach, startling the painted pelican into swimming an extra two feet out in the water.

True to his promise, in fifteen minutes, Digger stood on her doorstep.

He came in and looked around. "Nice," he said. "This should be just fine. Now, why don't we whip up those sandwiches and wrap them up. I've decided to take a long lunch hour again."

"Where are we going?"

"You'll see when we get there."

Quickly, she wrapped the sandwiches in wax paper and tucked them into a paper bag, then filled a thermos with coffee from the pot which during daytime hours was always plugged in.

Digger took her hand and the two of them ran down the path and to the beach. Once there, he led her to the jetty and a small motorboat. He pointed out into the bay to a small island. "We'll go there," he said.

He pulled the rope to start the motor, and they put-

putted their way across the bay. He pulled into a small inlet and beached the boat, then helped Cass out.

She let him. She was quite capable of leaping out on her own, but if Digger was intent on being a gentleman, she was sure willing to let him.

They sat on the white sand and ate their sandwiches. Lunch over, he said, "Let's explore, shall we?"

The beach appeared to surround the island. They both kicked off their shoes and wandered down it, walking where the water met the hard-ridged sand.

"Heavenly, isn't it?" Cass said.

"Yes. Now you know why I could never live anywhere but here."

"I understand," Cass said. "But you have a good job here. Maybe you could get an even better one in the city, but this is a good one, and you love it." He hadn't said the *m* word, but surely marriage was what that last comment had meant. She could be equally oblique. "If I lived here, there's nothing I could do but maybe work as a maid in the motel. There's a big difference between your future here and mine."

He didn't answer. They loitered on down the beach, occasionally stopping to look at shells.

They turned a corner. There, snugged up close to shore behind the island, was Jenkins' fishing boat.

Digger grasped Cass's hand and drew her backwards, out of sight range in case Jenkins himself were looking their way.

"So," he said when they'd withdrawn far enough to

avoid being seen or overheard, "this is where he holes up when he disappears. Where he lurks while waiting for his contact, or whatever."

The magic had left the day, with the presence of Jenkins on the sunwashed island.

Digger looked at his watch. "We might as well go," he said. "I've got to get back to work anyway."

After Digger went back to work, Cass returned to her trailer. Somehow, she had to put Jenkins out of business. If she'd ever doubted that Digger was right, those doubts were gone. There'd be no reason for Jenkins to lurk behind the island if he were running drugs, even if Dolphin Bay hadn't been the most unlikely spot in the whole world for that activity. But if he were capturing dolphins, it was perfect. When the dolphins left the beach, he could tail them, probably tossing a few fish overboard to encourage them to follow the boat. Then, out of sight, behind the island, he'd net one or two, contact the larger boat that would pick them up, and rendezvous where the eyes of the rangers couldn't see him.

She had no idea what the laws were regarding dolphins, but if he could sit in his boat in Dolphin Bay and capture them legally, he'd do that. Either it was illegal, or he thought it was. What she needed was to trick him, to operate her own sting, as it would be called in Los Angeles. She'd have to do it without Digger's knowledge, because he'd forbid her to have anything to do with it. For her own protection, he'd call it. She couldn't come up with a sting and leave Digger to carry it out, because Jenkins wouldn't trust him far enough to do anything shady if he were within a mile of the boat.

No. She was in this alone.

She poured a cup of coffee and sat at her table with a pen and notepad scribbling down ideas.

Could she pretend she wanted to buy one? No. That would put another dolphin in jeopardy. The best she could do was to continue as she'd started, to pretend she might want to but insist she couldn't decide without consulting Carl.

All right. Jenkins had told her to come back when she'd consulted her boss. She could pretend that Carl had expressed an interest, but had to talk money before deciding. That would give her an excuse for at least one more meeting without making a commitment.

She needed evidence of what Jenkins said beyond just her unsupported word. If she had a second person . . . Forget that. He'd have nothing to do with her if she had a second person along.

A tape-recorder maybe, a small one she could hide in her purse. Maybe Digger had one in his office. She could tell him that she wanted to record the dolphins.

She dumped the rest of her coffee in the sink, and left.

Digger was busy on his books.

"You have a tape-recorder?"

He leaned back in his chair and looked at her. "I'm not sure," he said. "Why? Why do you want one?"

"I thought I'd see if I could record the songs of the dolphins," she said. "You know, their sounds and squeaks." She tried a joke. "You never know, I might market it and have a best-seller on my hands."

He chuckled. "Well, we've got a fair amount of paraphernalia of one type or another around. Let's see what we can find." He moved to a row of cabinets and hunkered down in front of one of them. It was jammed with various and sundry radios and cameras and, yes, tape-recorders. He tossed three out on the floor.

"There you go," he said. "Take your pick."

One of them was the size of a suitcase. It was out. The other two were purse-sized. She checked them out, turning them on, counting, "Test, two, three, four," then running more tests by murmuring and whispering.

"I need a fairly sensitive one to pick up the dolphins," she said. One appeared to be definitely better than the other. "I'll try this one for now."

"Fine." Digger tossed the others back into the cupboard.

"Thanks." She took the tape-recorder and walked back to her trailer. Her purse was at the back of the closet in her bedroom. She rarely carried one, and it had been on the closet floor ever since she'd moved into the trailer. She proceeded to test the tape-recorder at different levels and distances and in her purse and out of it.

Even in the purse, it appeared to pick up low sounds at a reasonable distance. It would do just fine.

When would she put the plan into operation? Not today, that was for sure. The dolphins had already left by the time she and Digger had returned from lunch. She had to record some dolphin sounds to allay any suspicions Digger might have about why she needed a tape-recorder. Then she had to wait for Jenkins's boat to return to the jetty.

Tomorrow. Tomorrow she'd tape dolphins. The first chance she had after that, she'd tape herself and Jenkins. The sting operation. Would it stand up in court? She had no idea. But this much she was sure of: Jenkins wasn't the swiftest fish in the ocean. If she gave the tape to Digger, and Digger threatened Jenkins with it, he'd leave. Maybe he'd be a risk to other dolphins in other places, but the little community that frequented Dolphin Bay would be safe from him.

Next day, Cass stood in the water and taped dolphins. She was there with all the tourists, and after she recorded some squeaks and splashes, she played the tape back, for the children. They appeared enthralled. She'd have a child say, "Hi, dolphin," then record the first squeakings she could and play them back. "Listen," she'd say, "the dolphins are saying 'Hi' to you."

When she couldn't get squeaks, she'd use splashes. There were always lots of those.

Mainly, the activity was high profile, although it did also serve to get her comfortable with the machine so there'd be less chance of mistakes.

Afterwards, when the children and tourists had tired and the dolphins had begun to leave, she went to Digger's office.

"Hi," she said. "I've been taping."

He chuckled. "I noticed from the window. You seemed to be surrounded by children and dolphins both. Maybe when you finish, I'll keep the tape for ranger talks. Have you finished?"

"No. I want to do several days. Then I'll edit and leave you with the best one."

She took the machine and left. The next move would be to tape herself and Jenkins. The sting tape.

It was three days before Cass had the chance to try her tape-recorder with Jenkins. The first day, the boat was still absent. The second, it seemed that she couldn't get free of people who might notice what she was doing.

Finally on the third morning, Digger told her he'd be completely tied up until lunch as he was in a meeting with all the rangers but the one on tourist duty. Jon and Judy always spent their mornings writing. No one else paid any attention to what she did.

As before, she sauntered up the jetty, talking with

everyone she could find. No one could accuse her of furtive or suspicious movements. Even if she were observed chatting with Jenkins, he was just one more in a long series of contacts.

He greeted her, gave her coffee, tried to lure her into the front of the boat again, but was gracious when she refused.

"So, what's up?"

"Well," she said, "I've talked to my boss." She hoped he couldn't hear the sound of the tape turning. That was unlikely. It was a very quiet machine. She'd checked that carefully when she chose it.

"And?"

"He's interested, but he needs more information."

"Such as?"

"Such as how many dolphins could you supply in one trip?"

He shrugged. "One or two. Maybe three if one were a baby." He jerked his thumb toward the wading pool. "I've got to keep them in there. How many would he want?"

"Two probably," she said. "Just to replace ours that are getting older."

"Anything else he needs to know?"

"Probably an estimate on the price."

He named a sum. She came back with a lower one. They met halfway.

"So," he said, "want to place an order?"

"Not yet. I have to get back to my boss again. See

if the price is satisfactory. I'll contact you when I've heard."

"Do that."

She said her good-byes. That was good enough. She'd wait until she caught Digger in a good mood, tell him what she'd done and turn over the tape. He could take it from there. He'd be furious with her, but, after the fact, and when she'd returned in one piece, he'd undoubtedly not only forgive her, but be grateful to her.

She ambled back down the jetty, turning the recorder off to save the battery when she was far enough that Jenkins wouldn't see her.

"Coffee?" Digger asked when she came into his office, the way she usually did after her expeditions.

"Sure." She set her purse down beside her chair. They drank coffee and chatted, talking about the events of the day, discussing whether they'd go out to a restaurant for dinner or whether he'd cook, or she'd cook, or they'd cook together and at whose trailer.

When she asked about lunch, he shook his head. He'd brought sandwiches with him. If he worked through lunchtime, he said, he could book off early and go for a drive and have dinner somewhere further away. He went back to work and she left.

Digger worked at his computer. Every day, the rangers logged the numbers of dolphins, and, as far as possible, noted which individuals had appeared. Digger put the information on the computer, and analyzed it to establish trends.

He eventually got up to walk around the room and stretch. He noticed a purse, sitting on the floor. It was probably Cass's, but he'd better make sure and not return it to the wrong person. It could have been left by one of the women who had attended the morning meeting. He didn't recognize it. Most of the women here, including Cass, didn't carry purses. He didn't pay much attention to details like that anyway.

He opened it to look for identification. There was nothing in it but a tape-recorder. That meant it must belong to Cass. She'd borrowed one like it and had used it to tape dolphin noises, to say nothing of tourist noises and kid noises. She'd played them for him. He'd turn it on. If he recognized the squeaks and squeals, that would settle it and he'd return the thing to Cass when he got off work.

He turned it on. The dolphin squeaks and the children's excited voices appeared. He reached out to turn it off, then froze. The next voices were those of Cass and the man named Jenkins.

He listened to the conversation, stunned, then rewound the tape and played it again. Cass? His Cass? The woman he'd hoped to marry if he could only figure out how to get her gainfully employed in this place? She wouldn't agree otherwise. But here she was, on tape, negotiating with Jenkins to buy dolphins he captured. The woman he thought he loved was an unscrupulous fool. Unscrupulous, because she'd agreed with him about how terrible Jenkins was if he was capturing and selling dolphins. A fool, because it didn't take a rocket-scientist to figure out that, no matter what the selling price, these would be mighty expensive dolphins by the time she got them to Los Angeles.

She'd probably never get the scheme off the ground. Carl would have better sense whether she did or not. That didn't matter. What mattered was that he could never marry her now, could never love her. He'd have to have a showdown with her, tell her they were finished, and encourage her to hustle back to where she belonged as fast as possible. The only possible good to come if this was that he might be able to use the tape to threaten Jenkins so that the man would never show his face in Dolphin Bay again.

He slipped the tape out of the recorder and put it into the safe, then shut off the computer.

He might as well get this over with now. Delaying it would only mean more misery. He put the tape-recorder where it belonged, back in the cupboard, and picked up the empty purse.

He paused at her door before he knocked. Through the open screen door, he could see Cass, curled up on the sofa, asleep. She looked innocent as a baby. One arm curved above her head. The other rested along her side and hipbone. She was on her right side, the bottom leg stretched out, the top one bent at the knee.

She looked beautiful and vulnerable and desirable. He wished with all his heart that there were some reasonable explanation for what he'd found, but there couldn't possibly be.

He made a fist and knocked. Cass came to life slowly, stretching like a cat, then sitting up and rubbing her eyes. She saw him and came to the door. "Sorry," she said. "I was having an afternoon nap—a siesta. Come on in." She held the door open.

"I won't be long," he said. "I just came to return this." He held out the purse.

"Oh," she said, and shook her head as if still half-asleep. "You mean I left it. Sorry. I guess I'm just not used to carrying a purse."

She reached out and took it, then hefted it as if testing the weight. She looked into it and licked her lips nervously. "There was something in it," she said and hesitated. "Something I intended to give you."

"Yes," he said. "There was something in it all right, but I don't think you intended to give it to me. It already belonged to me. It was a tape-recorder."

"I know that," she said. "You want to sit down?" She gestured at the sofa.

Digger followed her gesture with his eyes. The sofa was still dented where she had lain. It looked warm and curved from the heat and shape of her body.

He grieved for what might have been.

"No," he said. "I don't want to sit down."

She swallowed, her eyes darting nervously from side to side. "Could I have the tape?"

"No, you can't. I'm keeping it for evidence."

"Of what?" She looked more and more like a trapped animal, searching frantically for a way out.

"Of Jenkins. Of you. Of what the two of you were up to."

"Listen," she said. "I did it for you. Honest. You suspected what Jenkins was doing, but you couldn't prove it. If you'd gone out to that boat, he'd have tipped any dolphins he had overboard before you had the evidence. I thought I'd run a sting. He didn't know I was connected to you. I thought if I pretended and taped our conversation, I could turn the tape over to you, and you could either turn it over to the authorities or at least use it to threaten him with so he'd leave."

"Then why didn't you give it to me? You had it in my office."

"You were busy," she said. "We were going out for dinner. I thought I'd turn it over when there was lots of time for me to explain."

"Sorry, Cass. What you're saying doesn't make any sense. I'd give anything if it were the truth, but I don't think it could be. Possibly. Yes, I'm going to use the tape against Jenkins. I think you'd better leave too. Just clear out and leave. Go back to Los Angeles. I'm sorry. This sure isn't what I had in mind when I invited you here."

"I can't leave," she said. "The date on my return

ticket is firm, and I've got this trailer rented for another couple weeks. If you'll just think about it, you'll
see I'm telling the truth. I'd have to be crazy otherwise. Can you imagine what it would cost to ship a
dolphin from here to California? If Carl had that kind
of money he wouldn't need a dolphin show." She
stomped over to a kitchen drawer and dug out a notepad. She wrote on it, then handed it to him. "Here.
That's Carl's phone number. Just phone him and ask.
Ask if he's heard anything about this. I made it all
up."

Digger stood in the doorway, propped up with one
elbow against the doorjamb. "If you'd lie to Jenkins,
you'd lie to me," he said. "And you'd ask Carl to lie
too. Sorry, Cass, it won't wash. If you refuse to leave,
I suppose I can't force you to, but it's over between
us. Goodbye."

He slammed the door as he left, and, once he was
out of Cass's sight, he brushed the beginning of tears
away. Australian men did not cry.

Chapter Seven

California women cried. Cass ran to her bedroom where prying eyes of bypassers would not see her through the door or window, and threw herself down on her bed. The tears came in a flood. Eventually she sat up, dried her eyes and thought about her options.

It wasn't fair. She'd just been trying to help Digger, in fact, had maybe risked her life to help him. He'd rewarded her by breaking off their relationship. She blew her nose.

She smiled grimly to herself. It sure wouldn't help to go to Jenkins and ask him to intercede for her. There was no point in trying to talk to Digger again. He'd made up his mind. The sensible thing would be to take Digger's advice and go home. But she wasn't a quitter, never had been, and she sure wasn't going to start now. Going home would be an admission of guilt.

She'd stay until her vacation was over. She'd go out and play with the dolphins as usual. If Digger didn't like it, he could simply lock himself in his office and ignore her. That sounded a lot like what he intended to do.

Maybe if she had someone to talk things over with. Judy. She'd tell Judy Brown her troubles. At worst, it might help her feel better. At best, Digger might listen to Judy, if she could just get Judy to believe her.

She washed her face, applied some makeup to cover the traces of tears and made her way to Jon and Judy's mobile.

They were home. "Could I talk to you?" she said to Judy.

"Come on in. What is it?"

Cass stayed in the doorway. "No," she said. "Alone."

"Jon and I don't have secrets. Anything I know, I'll tell him."

Cass swallowed. "That's okay," she said. "But I'll find it easier to talk if there's just you."

"Okay." Judy stepped out the door. "Be back soon," she said to Jon, and waved.

When they reached Cass's trailer, Judy put her arm around Cass and steered her to the table. "Just sit down," she said. "I think first, you need a nice hot cup of tea with lots of sugar in it. That's Jon's cure-all and it really helps. Now, just point at where it is."

"On the counter, in the canisters marked *tea* and *sugar*. The mugs are on that cup tree beside them."

"Thanks," Judy said cheerfully. "Stupid of me not to see them for myself."

They were silent as Judy made tea, brought it to the table and sat down opposite Cass. "Now, what's this all about?" she said.

Cass told her, haltingly, between sips of hot sweet tea, and ended by saying, "Besides that, he had no business listening to my tape."

Judy sat silent. "You know," she said finally, "I sort of know how Jack feels. Let me tell you a story. I've already sort of told you about it a bit, but now I'll give you the details. When Jon and I were travelling in New Zealand, and he was finally getting me convinced that he really and truly loved me, even though he still wouldn't tell me who he really was, I discovered a letter. We were at a bed and breakfast, and I went out to his camper to get the book I was working on. I discovered a letter from my dad, to Jon. I shouldn't have looked, but I did. I hadn't known my dad even knew Jon. In the letter he thanked Jon for looking after me and told him to submit an interim bill. Can you imagine? I was absolutely devastated. Here, I'd fallen in love with him and thought he was about to propose. Then I found out, I was nothing to him but the baby he was baby-sitting. For money yet. The whole thing had been planned between the two of them from the very beginning, right down to my itinerary."

"Well," Cass said, "you're married. You must have made it up."

Judy chuckled. "Yes," she said. "I intended to run off, but I slept late. He saw me and threw me over his horse, and carted me off to a law office in Christchurch. He stuck two coins into the parking meter for the horse and dragged me into the lawyer, where he asked him to draw up a fifty-thousand-dollar bond to show me he was serious about marrying me."

"And what did you do?"

Judy shrugged. "I had a major temper tantrum, and then I married him. What else could I do? I loved the guy."

Cass managed a weak smile. "Digg—uh, Jack's the one who needs to hear that story, I guess. I already know the truth."

Judy stood up, came around the table and hugged Cass. "Look," she said, "I'll talk this whole thing over with Jon. He looks a bit flamboyant, with his curls and his cut-off shorts, and his guitar, but he's got a lot of good common sense. We'll talk about what's best to do, and then most likely one of us will tackle Jack. Can you handle coming over for dinner?"

Cass shook her head. It had taken all her nerve to ask to talk to Judy, never mind having to make polite conversation with the two of them, knowing they were feeling sorry for her.

"I'm not quite up to it tonight," she said. "I'll just wallow in self-pity tonight."

"Lunch tomorrow then. Any time after twelve. If you really want to wallow, sleep late and call it brunch. Then the three of us can talk over things." She hugged Cass again. "Bye."

"Bye," Cass said weakly, then ran for the sanctuary of her bed.

"I think we should wait a couple days before I talk to Digger about your tape," Jon said at brunch.

Cass nibbled at her omelet, her bacon, and her toast. These were some of her favorite foods, but she sure didn't appreciate them now.

"We'll talk to him," Judy said. "Or, I think that Jon will. He'll tell him the story about the letter, and sympathize with his feelings. Jon's really very good at that sort of thing. He'll make him see reason."

"But I think we should give it a bit of time," Jon said. "Just to give him a chance to cool down and think things over. If he'll just think about it a bit, he'll see that your story makes a lot more sense than his theory does. You go about your normal life and play with your dolphins. If he really loves you, and I think he does, he'll start missing you, and start wondering. That will be the time for me to talk to him."

He reached out and tapped her on the chin with his closed fist. "Just hang in there, kid," he said, and then to Judy, "Give Cass another cup of coffee, darlin'."

* * *

The following morning, after her talk with Jon and Judy, Cass wanted to stay in her bed forever, to never move from the trailer bedroom. Maybe the whole thing was a bad dream and hadn't really happened. She pinched herself. Not a dream.

She'd take Jon's advice, in fact, do what she'd resolved to do from the beginning, and go about her normal life. She struggled to the kitchen and made herself coffee and nuked a muffin. Then she dressed in her perkiest navy shorts and her brightest red T-shirt. She wasn't going to let the world know she'd died inside.

The dolphins were coming in when she reached the beach. She scanned them for her favorites. Bugsy was there, and Joan, and Bubbles. She didn't see Darby anywhere. She'd probably arrive shortly.

Cass bought fish, kicked off her sandals and waded into the water. She fed Bugsy. She fed Joan. She had only two fish left, and Darby still hadn't appeared.

Several tourists were in the water with their buckets of fish.

"Oh, look," a little girl said to her father, "look, Daddy." She pointed at Joan and Bubbles. "Look," she said, "there's a mummy and baby." Joan took the fish the child offered, but, like Darby before her, kept between the tourists and Bubbles.

"No," the ranger on duty said, "actually that isn't the baby's mother. The baby's mother doesn't seem to be here at the moment. She's probably out fishing. Dolphins share child-care duties just like people do."

"Do they really?" The child was obviously impressed with this bit of information.

The ranger didn't seem to be at all concerned about Darby's absence. Maybe he was right. Maybe there was nothing to be concerned about. Darby would probably appear any moment.

Cass scratched and patted Joan, and watched the tourists. Eventually the tourists left. Then the dolphins left. Darby still had not appeared. Cass left the water and wandered onto the jetty. Jenkins's boat wasn't in its normal spot.

Cass turned cold all over. The coincidence was too much. The last thing she could bear was the thought of facing Digger with this information. He'd undoubtedly blame her, think she'd asked Jenkins to capture Darby. However, she couldn't keep her suspicions to herself. If Darby didn't reappear next time the dolphins came in, Digger would have to net Bubbles and attempt to feed her.

As for Darby, ideas for rescuing her were brewing in Cass's mind. She'd have to work alone or at least appear to. If she didn't manage to sneak in quietly enough, at least she'd have an excuse for coming, would just tell Jenkins that she'd come for the next meeting. Then, even if she weren't able to rescue Darby, once she was sure Jenkins had her, she could turn that information over to Digger, so he could alert the authorities.

Grimly, she left the beach, marched into the tourist center and rapped on his office door.

"Come in," Digger called, and glanced up briefly as Cass entered the room. She stood uncertainly in the open doorway.

When he saw who it was, he jumped to his feet, and leaned over his desk, hands splayed on the top. "I thought I made things very clear to you the other day. Why have you come in here?"

A muscle at the side of his mouth twitched.

Cass tried not to look at him, at the blue eyes, at the tic that gave away his vulnerability. She closed the door, and forced herself across the few feet of floor that divided her from his anger, then sank uninvited into the chair in front of his desk, distraught but dry-eyed.

She folded her hands into a knot of tension in her lap, and for a moment kept her eyes on the interlaced fingers. Then she looked unwillingly up to meet the burning anger in his eyes. He'd be sure to think that what she was about to say was proof of her guilt.

She took a deep breath before she spoke. "I'm sorry you're angry at me, Digger. I haven't done anything wrong, so you've no right to hate me. I told you the truth about the tape. But right now, we have to forget all of that. Darby's missing, and we have to help Bubbles."

The muscles rippled on his jaw line as he clenched and released his teeth.

"What trick are you up to now? Am I going to be treated to a session of crocodile tears?"

She shook her head and gazed at him, unflinching.

"So Darby's missing, is she?"

Just as she'd thought. He immediately blamed her.

"Yes. The others were in this morning. Joan was taking care of Bubbles. Darby didn't appear at all. I looked up the jetty and Jenkins' boat wasn't there."

Digger sighed in exasperation and sat down. "So what do you know about this? Did you put in an order for Darby?"

"No," she said. "I didn't. If you stop to think about this you'd know that. If I'd done that, why would I be here now?" She sat down across from him and looked at him earnestly. "Just think about it. If either of us are responsible for this, it's you. If you'd believed me the other day and taken the tape and used it against Jenkins, Darby would be safe now, and so would Bubbles."

"So what makes you so sure Jenkins has her? There are sharks and boat propellers and fishermen's nets." He held a yellow octagonal pencil between his fingers, tapping first the point, then the eraser, on top of his desk, sliding the length of the pencil through his fingers each time. Cass looked at the strong, brown, capable hands, and envied the pencil. It, at least, received attention from him.

She looked down at her own hands, still lying clenched in a little knot on her lap. "It's just a pretty strong coincidence that she's gone and Jenkins's boat is gone at the same time. Can't you send out the coast guard or something?"

He spoke quietly, but his tension showed in the way he tapped the pencil end more restlessly. "No," he said. "Not unless we have more evidence than the fact that a dolphin is missing."

She had a sudden inspiration. It couldn't do any harm. If he turned her down, she could still sneak out on her own. Besides, the way he felt about her now, he probably wouldn't care if she were in danger.

She leaned toward him. "I've got an idea," she said. "Yeah?"

"Well, we've got a pretty good idea where his boat is, don't we? Around behind the island."

"So?"

"So, we wait until the middle of the night and take that motorboat of yours and go out there. We'll try to sneak in quietly, but if he hears us, I'll just pretend that I hired somebody to bring me out. On the tape, if you remember, I'd spoken of another meeting. Now if we sneak in, we can release Darby. If he hears us, I'll go on the boat by myself and do another song and dance about Carl, and having to call him again before I can say for sure. Maybe I'll say that he has to arrange for the rest of the shipping first. But I'll know then whether she's there, and if she is, we can come back and you can send the Coast Guard or whoever to free her."

He snapped the pencil he'd been worrying around the desk, and threw the pieces down. "It sounds pretty risky for you."

"Not really. I've talked to him on his boat twice before. Please. We've got to do something. For Bubbles. I know you can keep her alive for awhile on artificial milk if you can net her tomorrow. But not forever. Please, Digger. Please." She permitted herself a weak smile. "Besides," she said, "I've got you. You can rescue me."

He leaned back in his chair and eyed her speculatively, silently, for a moment, then made his decision. "All right. If Bubbles comes in with Joan tomorrow, and Darby still isn't here, I'll go down and net Bubbles. We can always release her, but if we wait to capture her, our chance may be gone. We'll try to bottle feed her, but I doubt if we'll be successful for very long. Dolphin milk is very rich, and I don't think regular milk will do much for her. If she were older, we might be able to save her. But, yes, we have to do something."

Cass unfolded her hands and stirred, ready to get out of her chair.

"Just a minute," he said. "The rest of your plan. I'll have to give that more thought. Why can't I go by myself?"

"Think about it. I've got an excuse for going. You don't. He looks like a person who'd carry a gun."

"That's supposed to make me feel better about letting you do this?"

"He's not going to shoot me. I'll pretend it's another interview."

"Yeah, right. At two o'clock in the morning."

At least he was starting to consider it. She smiled. "We can go at three," she said, "if you think that's better."

In the end, they went at eleven. Even Jenkins wouldn't be stupid enough to believe that Cass had come out to negotiate business at two or three in the morning.

Cass dressed carefully, in black jeans, sweater, socks, and shoes. She tied a dark scarf over her hair, and tucked a sharp knife into her belt in case there were ropes over Darby that she'd have to cut. The night was moonless, black as pitch, with only the stars, dominated by the Southern Cross, piercing the curtain of the velvet sky. Not a breath of wind stirred; the night sat as still and heavy as the dark waters of the bay. Cass circled the campground and the tourist center, hoping to get on the jetty unseen in her black clothes. She succeeded, and walked up the jetty to the boat.

"Digger," she called softly.

"Here," came a whisper almost at her elbow. He was dressed in black too, moving as smoothly and silently as a cat.

"All set?"

They made their way up the jetty and untied the motorboat.

"Digger?" she whispered.

"Yes."

"One more thing. Jenkins isn't a very nice person. If he hears us, you get back in the boat and keep your head down. I'll handle him."

"Oh, yeah, right. I'm just going to cower in the boat and let you face the music." There was a distinct edge to his voice. "Australian men don't do that, baby."

"Please. Otherwise you'll put us both in danger. If I need your help, you can always come to my rescue."

"No promises, Cass. I'm not used to taking shelter while the women go out to fight. We'll play it by ear."

She settled herself in the boat, listening to the strong throbbing of the motor as Digger steered. She wasn't worried about his finding the way. He knew this area, land and sea, like the back of his hand.

Before long, the blacker blackness of the island loomed against the darkness of the night sky. Digger throttled the motor back to keep the noise down. They crept around the side of the island.

Jenkins's boat was where she and Digger had seen it that day they'd picnicked on the island, riding at anchor in a calm sea. Cass had no trouble finding it. Her eyes had become accustomed to the darkness on the ride out.

All was quiet. No lights showed on the boat. If Jenkins had heard them, he gave no sign. Digger used the oars to nose the small boat silently up against the large one. He tied it loosely, so that if they needed to take off in a hurry, they had only to jump into the boat and pull the end of the rope to undo the knot. He then leaped onto the deck silently on rubber-soled shoes, and held out his hand to help Cass.

"We're in luck," Digger whispered. "I think he's sleeping."

Cass looked around the deck. The plastic swimming pool lay close to the railing, with something dark in it and a tangle of ropes over the top.

Cass and Digger tiptoed closer. "It's Darby," she whispered.

The dolphin began to stir.

"Hush," Cass said, putting out her hand to pat the dolphin. "Be quiet. We're here to help you."

Darby stilled as if she understood.

Cass slid out her knife, and, when Digger held out his hand, gave it to him. After all, he'd make faster work of the ropes.

He cut them quickly.

"Okay, old girl, just be still," she murmured to Darby. Both she and Digger stepped into the pool beside the dolphin. Cass slipped her arms under Darby toward the back, and Digger grasped her under the middle.

"One, two, three," Cass whispered, and they both lifted. Somehow, Darby too seemed to give a mighty lunge to help them, and on the first try she slipped over the side of the boat and into the water below. Digger and Cass scrambled from the pool and started to leave, but the splash had brought Jenkins running.

"What's going on here?"

Digger grabbed Cass's hand, and they ran for the back. The knife clattered to the floor. Jenkins dashed for the front of the boat.

Digger stood poised to jump into the motorboat, Cass close behind him.

Suddenly Jenkins's boat leaped forward. He'd already made it to the controls. Digger, partly in the motorboat, fell the rest of the way. The rope holding the two boats together snapped with the impact. Cass fell back, onto the deck of Jenkins's boat.

Then Jenkins was back. His boat, on automatic pilot, headed away from the island and out to the open sea.

"Hold it. What's going on here?"

Cass scrambled to her feet and faced Jenkins. Her escape route was gone. She might as well make the best of a bad job.

"She escaped," she said. "I came out to talk to you again, and then I saw you already had a dolphin. I took off the ropes to get a better look, and she escaped. I'm sorry."

Jenkins grabbed her arm and bent it up. "Who's with you?"

"Nobody," Cass said. "I just came out to talk to you again. I told you that."

"If nobody's with you, how come somebody jumped into that boat, and now it's suddenly following us?"

Cass looked over the back of the boat. Sure enough, Digger's motorboat gave chase, falling farther and farther behind.

"I just hired a guy to drive the boat," she said.

"I'm sure you did. Now why did you really come here?"

He waited.

"I already told you," she said.

He jerked the arm he was holding upwards.

"Look, Doll, you don't play games with me. The truth?"

Where were her self-defense skills when she needed them? All she could think of was how much her arm hurt.

She faced him boldly. "All right," she said. "I'll tell you what I was really doing. I came out to free the dolphin. When I came out last time, I was on a sting operation. I'm sure you know what that means. The tape is in the vault back at Dolphin Bay, and if anything happens to me, my friend will do more with it than just keep you from stealing dolphins."

He released her arm.

Now she was free, maybe she could overpower him. She took a step backward. He grabbed her arm again.

"For your sake, I hope you swim better than you bargain."

Before she had time to think about the self-defense skills she was so proud of, he'd grabbed her legs and propelled her headfirst over the side of the boat. "Now, why don't you just go join your dolphin friends unless your boyfriend rescues you!"

As Cass hit the water, she heard the big boat surge forward even faster with a mighty roar of engines.

Digger had landed flat on his back when the big boat surged forward. He scrambled up, ready to jump back on deck and do battle. Unless Cass was right about the gun, he could overpower any sixty-some hippie ever put on this earth. He'd have to be careful about getting back on to give him the element of surprise.

The boat had left. The rope he'd tied up with was only a frayed end. It was his fault. He should never have listened to Cass's outlandish plan.

Unless he'd been set up, and this had all been planned. He almost hoped so. At least that way Cass would be alive.

No. It was an irrational idea. Cass had told him the truth. Her actions tonight proved that.

He rubbed his back where he'd hit it on the seat when he tumbled. Then he made his way back to the motor. There was nothing for it but to try to catch Jenkins's boat. His common sense told him he could best help Cass by going back to Dolphin Bay and alerting the authorities. He couldn't bring himself to do that. It would be turning his back on her in her hour of need to calmly head back to safety.

He started the motor and revved it up to top speed. He wasn't sure what he'd do if he caught the larger boat. It didn't matter. Jenkins' boat got further away with every passing second. Chasing it was a futile gesture.

He thought he heard a splash and a distant cry, but he couldn't be sure. Had she gone overboard, either pushed or jumped, or had Jenkins taken off with her? He was unsure of what to do. If she were overboard, obviously he had to circle around and find her, if that was possible in this dark night.

On the other hand, if she were still in the boat it was imperative to get back and alert the law as soon as possible, so that Jenkins wasn't completely out of reach. He realized he could never catch the boat, and if he did, had no way of boarding it. Both boats had already moved a considerable distance from the island, and in the darkness it was hard to know in exactly what direction, although he knew they'd gone further out to sea.

He would look for her for fifteen minutes, then go to shore and report her missing. The police would go after Jenkins' boat with helicopters. Boats with search-lights would scour the bay for Cass.

He started the motor and chugged slowly in the di-rection that Jenkins' boat had gone, cutting the motor every few minutes and shouting into the darkness. Once he thought he heard an answering cry in the distance, but when he called again there was only si-lence. He nosed the boat toward the direction the sound had come from, but there was nothing there and no answer to his calls. The first answer had probably been an echo or else his imagination.

He circled again and again, stretching his original fifteen minutes into thirty, then reluctantly left the area. He had to alert the police, and get a search started.

When Digger reached Dolphin Bay, he beached the boat and phoned the authorities. That was all well and good, but he couldn't bear not doing what he could.

He pounded on the door of the Browns's mobile, and when Jon answered, wearing jeans that had been flung on in a moment, told him the whole story.

"The police will look for the boat," he said. "But I can't just sit here. Will you come with me and help me search?"

"Give me a minute," Jon said. "Why don't you grab

a canoe? It's quieter, and cuts out the risk of running her down. Leave the speedboat stuff to the police."

They stopped only for flashlights and binoculars. Within a short time, almost as fast as the motorboat at its lowest speed, they had, with driving strokes, brought the canoe into the area where Cass had disappeared.

Throughout the night, they circled, shining the flashlight over the water, calling Cass's name and hoping that the speedboats around them with the searchlights were having better luck. When dawn broke, they scanned the empty sea with binoculars, then headed the canoe back to the jetty and in the gray light of early morning crossed the north side of the beach and entered the tourist center.

"It's no use any more," Digger said. "She couldn't possibly be still swimming around there after all this time."

Chapter Eight

After Jenkins threw her overboard, Cass was stunned for a few seconds, then dived to get out of the way of the boats until they had passed beyond her.

She surfaced, shaking the water from her eyes. The night was inky dark, and she could see the lights of the fishing boat disappearing into the distance, Digger's boat still following it.

When Digger realized he'd never catch the other boat, he'd surely come back. She began to swim in the direction of the receding boats. She heard Digger's motor when he quit chasing Jenkins and began to circle. That meant he'd heard her go overboard, and was moving slowly to look for her and to avoid hitting her. Periodically she heard the motor stop, and she heard his voice in the distance calling, "Cass."

"Here," she shouted, and waved one arm. "Over here."

The voice came again, calling, "Cass."

She opened her mouth to answer, but got a mouthful of water from the wake of the boat. She coughed and sputtered, then called, "Here, over here." But the motor had started again. Had he located her or hadn't he heard her?

The boat circled her. Her eyes had long ago become adjusted to the darkness and the moon had begun to rise. She could see the boat clearly, with Digger silhouetted against the night. She raised her arm from the water and waved.

She'd worn a close-fitting black sweater to avoid being seen on the jetty. It was probably keeping Digger from seeing her now. She struggled out of it, not easy in the water, and by time she surfaced the boat was out of sight again. Then she saw its lights and started to swim toward it.

She would have done better to have forgotten about rescue, and swum toward shore. The salt water was buoyant, the night was calm, she was a strong swimmer and could probably have made it if she had taken it easy and rested often. Unless the sharks found her. There were many sharks in this area. But the moment of hysteria was replaced with logic. There was no reason for her to attract sharks or for them to attack her. She hadn't been injured in the sense of leaving trails of blood.

However, she had spent time and strength swimming around and around after the motor boat, and she was exhausted and beginning to panic. After all her fuss about her job and her condo, was it all going to end with her dying out here at the age of twenty-six?

"No, Cass," she said to herself. "Don't panic. Don't think about dying. Just swim to shore, slowly and calmly."

Panic was fatal. She knew that. Once she started thrashing about wildly, she was done. She would drown, and, even if she didn't, she would raise her chances of being found by sharks. Animals could smell fear, and she was sure that sharks could too. She took a deep breath, kicked off her jeans, and floated on her back to rest.

"Dear God," she prayed to a being that she had never in her whole life given a thought to, "bring me through this, and I'll work for charity, and I'll go to church, and I'll always be kind to people and animals."

She opened her eyes, and saw the tip of a fin moving toward her. Terror set in.

They've come. The sharks. Against all reason, she opened her mouth and screamed.

Something nudged her side. She thrashed about wildly and screamed again.

Whatever had touched her side was nuzzling her. Gently. This was no shark. The animal surfaced and breathed. Then she knew.

"Darby," she breathed. "Darby. You've come to save me."

She rested her hand against Darby's back, and her tears mixed with the night, and the sea.

They stayed a moment like that, and then Darby started moving around, rubbing against Cass. Then she swam under her, and came up between her legs.

Suddenly Cass understood. She'd read stories from ancient Greece of men riding dolphins, and today's legends making the rounds told of a sailor, a diver, a shipwrecked fisherman, who had been brought to shore on the back of a dolphin. Nobody ever heard these stories from the people they'd happened to—just from friends of friends of friends, or from someone who'd heard the story from a nameless sailor talking in a bar.

Regardless of, or perhaps because of, her knowledge of dolphins, Cass had never believed these stories, but now she knew. The stories were true, and Darby had come to save her.

Gratefully, she clenched her legs around Darby's body, and clutched the dorsal fin, as if she were riding a horse and grasping the saddle horn.

Darby took off through the water, not as fast as the dolphins in the stories, almost as if she understood that Cass's strength was ebbing, and that she wouldn't be able to hold on at full speed.

Somehow, during the ride, the strength seemed to flow from Darby to Cass. Although Cass originally feared that she could never stay on long enough to ever see Dolphin Bay again, as the journey went on she found herself sitting straighter and not grabbing the fin with quite the same desperation.

Darby swam into the familiar beach, where she was used to bringing her baby every morning. She came in as close as she dared without beaching herself, then turned sideways gently, spilling Cass off into the sand and shallow water. There she hovered, watching anxiously as Cass crawled up onto the sandy beach, the one where the dolphins came, across the jetty from the beach used by boats.

Once Cass was safely out of the water, Darby slapped her tail on the surface and disappeared. Finally safe, Cass collapsed onto the beach, and slept, clad only in her wet underclothes, through the chill of the desert night.

That was where Digger and Jon found her—on the dolphins' beach.

When they'd got back from searching, Judy had coffee ready for them, then insisted that, useless as it seemed, they get in the canoe and search again.

"She's a strong swimmer," Judy had said. "She told me that. The water's warm and if she doesn't panic she can float and swim indefinitely. Now, you two just get back out there and look."

"Let's check the dolphins' side of the beach," Digger said. "Regardless of everything else, if the dolphins are in I have to do something about netting Bubbles."

They almost stumbled over her, lying prone in the sand.

"It's Cass," Jon said, then more soberly he asked, "Is she alive?"

They forgot about the canoe. They even forgot about the dolphins. Digger hunkered down and shook Cass by the shoulder.

"Cass, wake up! It's Digger. Come on, Cass."

She stirred in the sand. A great feeling of relief washed over him and he hated himself for his earlier doubts about her. She'd freed Darby, and had nearly died doing it.

Laboriously, Cass pushed herself to a sitting position. It was difficult. She hurt all over. Her muscles were sore, and she had knife-like pains in her chest and side. It even hurt to breathe.

I'm stiff from lying here all night, she thought. *But once I move around, it'll be all right. And Jon and Digger are here.* She heard Jon say, "Here they come. They're early."

"Joan and Bubbles are here," Digger said. "I don't see Darby yet."

Just then Darby swam into the midst of the little group of dolphins.

The dolphins crowded around her, and there were little whistling sighs of joy and greeting.

Then Darby slid next to Joan and reclaimed her baby.

"Oh, it's Darby," Cass cried. "I've got to thank her." She stumbled to her feet and, ignoring the pain, through the sand and into the water. Digger followed her closely.

"Thank you, Darby," she cried, "oh, thank you. Dear, dear Darby."

And then Darby, dear Darby, swam through the water, and touched Cass gently with her beak.

Cass's knees would no longer hold her up, and she felt herself sagging into the water. Then, she was in Digger's arms, being carried over the beach, and she didn't remember any more.

The days passed in a fog for Cass. There was pain, but then there was a drugged stupor that made the pain bearable. She had moments of semi-awareness, and through these Digger and Jon and Judy and a kindly gray-haired man who said, "There, there," and jabbed needles into her seemed to swim in and out of her consciousness like figures in a dream.

In the dream, Cass was turned and rubbed and dressed and undressed and washed. Judy was always there, doing these things for her. Glassy-eyed and stunned, Cass resisted Digger and Jon as they forced pills down her, and made her drink water and broth. All she wanted was to sink back down into her lethargy and sleep, and when they propped her up for the pills and fluids, she shook her head at them like a sick calf and struggled weakly to push them away.

She had dreams about dying and God and dolphins and Darby and promising God how good she'd be if only he didn't let her drown. Sometimes in the middle of these dreams, she would wake up drenched with sweat, tossing, and babbling aloud. The babbling was all mixed up with the sleep and the dreams and she wasn't sure how much she dreamed and how much she really said.

Whenever she awoke, Digger or Jon or Judy was always there, one of them, sitting at her bedside, or at the table across the room, head propped on a weary arm, reading and drinking coffee to stay awake through the lonely night. The moment she stirred, the vigil keeper was at her side, soothing her, bathing her with lukewarm water, changing her sweat-soaked nightshirt and sheets for ones that were crisp and clean.

If she continued to toss and turn, one of them would hold her hand and murmur soothing words until she drifted back into her clouded sleep.

The days and nights were a confused jumble of a comatose sleep, mixed with a foggy awareness of someone patting her and saying, "There, there, Cass, you'll be all right." Sometimes when her fevered twistings brought her partially out of her oblivion, Judy would already be bathing her with tepid water or Digger would be holding damp cloths on her forehead.

They even made occasional attempts to brush her hair, but her head would roll limply like Raggedy Ann's, and they would have to give it up. She thought vaguely that she should have been embarrassed at wasting all their time, when Digger should have been watching the dolphins and Jon and Judy should have been writing. She was really too tired to think about it, and anyway it was all a dream.

Finally, on a bright blue morning, she came out of her dream. The sun was streaming into the caravan, and all the windows were open to catch every bit of breeze. The yellow and brown print curtains stirred softly with each breath of air drawn in by the opened windows. Cass could smell salt water on the air, and she knew she was alive, really and truly alive, rather than swimming, zombie-like, up to a lesser level of stupor. Her body was cool instead of burning, and, although she was still weak, she felt that she was once more alive and aware upon the earth. The lethargy had gone.

She knew she had passed some sort of turning point and that she was not going to die. She was very much alive and she was lying in her own bed in her rented trailer. The sheets were clean, and she was wearing her own cotton nightshirt and it was clean. Something that smelled really good simmered on the stove. Through the open door, she could see Digger sitting at the kitchen table reading.

She sat right up, on her own, looked across at Digger and said, "Hi, Digger! That smells good. I'm hungry."

Digger slammed his book shut and, in two seconds, was on his knees beside her. "You're back! You've come back to us. Oh, Cass, you've been through so much. Please forgive me for ever doubting you."

She reached out and touched his hand. "There's nothing to forgive, Digger," she said. "I should have given you the wretched tape the moment I got back from making it, and all this would have been prevented."

He raised her hand to his lips and kissed it. "Honey," he said, "you're going to live and that's all that matters. Now, I've got to tell Jon and Judy. Excuse my yelling. I don't want to leave you long enough to go to their place."

He stood in the doorway and shouted. "Jon, Judy, come here."

Jon and Judy arrived a moment later, red-faced from running. "What's wrong?" Judy was out of breath and gasping. "Is Cass worse?"

"No, no. She's okay. She's awake. She's okay."

Judy glanced through the open door. Cass waved weakly. Judy threw her arms around Digger, and Jon threw his arms around both of them.

"All right, you guys," Cass said. "Can't I get in on the hugging and kissing?"

They started toward the bed. "No," she said. "You're going to do all that after I'm up. You guys just step outside. All of you," she said, as Digger started toward her.

"Come on," Judy said. "Let's do as she wants. We'll be right outside if there's a problem."

Cass watched them leave and close the door. She was determined to get out of bed on her own. Carefully, she placed her hands by her sides and, throwing her weight on them, eased herself to a full sitting position, back propped against the wall at the head of the bed. She moved her hands from under the covers. They looked thin and white. The blue tracery of the veins stood out clearly against the pallor of her wrist.

These were not her hands, couldn't be her hands. Her hands weren't pallid and shaky. They were firm and brown and strong. The hand she used to carefully throw back the sheet and blanket that covered her was pallid and shaky.

Cautiously she turned and swung her legs over the side of the bed. Her legs were white and shaky too, like the legs of an old woman. She placed her hands carefully at her side and pushed herself into a standing position. The world spun around her, and her white legs, as weak as water, shook and trembled. She collapsed on the side of the bed. It was no use. She couldn't stand up. She was as wobbly as a newborn foal. If she had tried to take a step, or even stay on her feet, she'd have fallen. It was better for them to come back and find her still in bed than in a crumpled heap on the floor. She sat a moment, panting, collecting up her little strength and then carefully she drew her legs back up onto the bed. Her feeble hands tugged the sheet and blanket back up over her legs.

"You can come in now," she called in a voice that was little more than a whisper.

They filed back in. Digger sat down carefully on the side of the bed, facing her, and cupped her face in his hands. "Oh, Cass," he said. "You're all right. You're really all right. The doctor said you would be."

"But I can't stand up," she said. "I tried to stand up and I couldn't."

"That doesn't matter. You're just weak from being in bed so long." He stroked her face as if to reassure himself. "You're all right."

"I'm hungry," she said. "Could I have some of whatever's on the stove that smells so good?"

From the corner of her eye, she saw Judy poke Jon in the ribs. "We're leaving now," Judy said. "Call me if she needs me for anything."

"Thanks." Digger turned back to Cass. "I was just making some beef stew," he said. "I've been making my meals and eating here so I don't have to be away as much. You can have a bit of the broth. You'll make yourself sick if you eat a lot right now. You can have some broth now, and then I'll give you a bit more in an hour or so."

He stepped into the tiny kitchen, took a mug from the cup stand on the counter, and spooned some of the broth from the stew into it, then sat by Cass. He supported her with his right arm around her thin shoulders, as he held the cup with his left hand, letting her have a small sip at a time.

She drank the broth eagerly, feeling strength flowing into her with every sip, and, when it was finished, she asked for more.

"No," he said, "that's it for now, my girl. It's back to sleep for you, and we'll give you a bit more when you wake up."

She was tired. She was tired from the effort of sitting up in bed, tired from her abortive attempt to stand, tired from concentrating on drinking from the mug. But the exhaustion was healthy and normal, the fatigue that comes from driving a weak body too fast.

Thankfully, she slid back down into bed, falling into a natural sleep while Digger watched.

He'd been lucky, Digger thought. Her not drowning the night of Darby's rescue was a major miracle. Her recovery from the ensuing illness was another miracle.

Aside from loving her, he could never have shed his guilt if she'd died or suffered permanent damage. It was his fault. The whole thing was his fault. His mistakes were legion. First, he should never have listened to the tape. He'd been ninety percent sure the purse was hers. Why hadn't he just taken it to her? Once he had listened to the tape, why hadn't he believed her explanation and immediately used the tape for its original purpose—to get Jenkins off the premises? He'd been wrong again when he'd let Cass talk him into the rescue operation. He should have taken Jon and a couple of rangers with him and gone to Jenkins's boat himself. If Darby hadn't been there, they could have just said they'd been in the area and decided to stop in to say hello.

However, he did love her and wanted to marry her. He was sure that she loved him. She'd never have come here otherwise. His concern was the same as hers—how could he ask this young vibrant highly educated woman to settle down to a life of cooking his meals and washing his socks? How long could love survive these conditions?

Cass's recovery was fast. She had, after all, not only been young and healthy, but extraordinarily healthy. As Digger had told the doctor, she didn't drink or smoke, she ate well, and she normally ran between one and two hours every day.

She ate a bit every few hours and gained strength. The second morning, she got out of bed with Digger's help and sat for a while at the table. She alternated naps with periods of sitting up and walking around with Digger's support. By the end of the day she was walking by herself.

That evening, she sat up in bed. Digger sat on the bed beside her gently brushing her hair, trying to bring some sort of order to the mess of salt-caked tangles.

"What was wrong with me?" she asked him. "The

last thing I remember is Darby greeting me, and then I collapsed."

"You had pneumonia," he said. "When we found you on the beach you weren't wearing anything but your underclothes. We assume you'd been there most of the night. Somehow you must have managed to swim back and then collapsed. We were out looking for you all night and if we'd walked over to the dolphin's beach we'd have found you when we got back. After that swim you must have been exhausted, and then after lying out all night with nothing on—and these desert nights can get pretty cool."

"Yes," she said. "The beach. I remember I was so tired and I lay down on the beach, just for a moment. But you'd looked for me. You drove your boat around, and then you went away. You came back?"

"Yes. Jon came with me. We took a canoe. Before morning there was a full-scale search on the go. But you'd have already been back on the beach. You swam in to the dolphin's beach. All the action was on the public side, the side the boats use. No one thought of looking on the dolphins' side."

"I don't know about the canoe. But you did your best with the boat. I heard you out there, but I had on dark clothes, and when I called, you couldn't hear me."

"I know that," Digger said. "I know that now."

"I got out of the clothes," she said, "but by that time it was too late. You'd gone."

He gave up on the hair, leaving most of the tangles in their matted clumps. He dropped the brush onto the floor beside him, and rotated his hand gently between Cass's shoulder blades.

"You're a pretty gutsy woman," he said huskily, "to have made your way back, by yourself."

Her eyes filled with tears. "It was terrible," she said. "I swam around in circles trying to chase the boat. I thought I was going to die. I've never been so terrified in my life."

She paused for a moment, as if to collect her thoughts. "And then," she said, "when it was the very worst, I saw a fin. It was moving toward me, coming at me. I thought it was a shark and I started screaming and couldn't stop. But it wasn't a shark. It was Darby. I didn't swim back. It was Darby. Darby rescued me."

"What do you mean?" He looked at her sideways, as if she were delirious again. "You want to explain this? How could Darby rescue you?"

"She did," Cass insisted, as she moved to look into his blue eyes with her golden ones. "Like I told you, I kept swimming around following your boat. I could hear you calling, and I kept calling, but you couldn't hear me, probably because of the motor. I tired myself, and I thought I was going to drown, and then I thought, 'I'm going to die out here and I'm only twenty-six' and then I said to God—

"Yes, God," she repeated firmly in response to his uplifted eyebrow, continuing to look at him steadily.

"I know I've never really spent a lot of time chatting with God before. We weren't even acquaintances. But, yes, I told God that if he'd just get me out of this one, I'd go to church and do good works, and always be kind to people and animals. And then I felt something nudge me, and there was Darby."

Digger's hand stopped the rotating movements, but he kept it still against her back, supporting her, almost holding his breath, waiting for the rest of this impossible story.

"She slithered around so that I knew she wanted me to get on her back and I did, and I held onto her fin, and she brought me here, and stayed until I'd crawled up on the beach. And that's the last I knew until you woke me up and I had this terrible pain in my chest and I waded into the water to thank Darby and then I passed out."

Digger sat in silence for a moment. Then he pulled Cass gently to him and held her in his arms, and she rested her cheek against his chest, feeling the warmth of his body through the brown cotton of his shirt.

"I'd heard stories like that," he said, "but I really never believed them."

"I know," she whispered. "Neither did I. But it happened. It really did. I'm not lying."

"I never said you were."

"And Jenkins? What about Jenkins?"

"No worries," Digger said. "He was picked up the next day, and is sitting in jail awaiting trial. Your tape will be a major piece of evidence. Now," he said as he eased her back down onto the bed, "I think you'd better get back to sleep."

He ran his hand over the back of her neck and up into her hair. Then he kissed her hair.

"Good night, sweet girl," he whispered.

Chapter Nine

"**S**o what happened while I was sick?" Cass asked Judy the next day. "Jack started to tell me, and then we got talking about other things."

"Well," Judy said, "you had pneumonia. We brought you up here to your caravan and called the doctor. He examined you and said you had pneumonia, but that you seemed as strong as an ox, and you'd probably pull through."

"Oh, yes," Cass said, "my caravan. I keep forgetting to call it that. I just call it a trailer. And I keep forgetting that Digger's real name is Jack, and I just keep calling him Digger. I don't really have it together, do I?"

Judy laughed. "I don't think it matters much," she said. "Caravan, camper-van, trailer, mobile—who cares? And I think you could call Digger a two-headed kangaroo and he'd still love you."

"Love me?"

"Yes. Love you. And as far as having it together, I think you've got it very much together. I don't think of myself as a shrinking violet, but I could never have gone out to that—that—that ape's boat with a hidden tape recorder. Never, ever, in my wildest dreams could I have done what you did." She snickered. "Mind if I put it in a book?"

"That's another thing," Cass said. "I've kept you all from your work."

"It wasn't anything. We all took turns. But Digger took the most. Anyway, between us, we seemed capable of giving you such good care that the doctor saw no reason to move you to a hospital. Then he pumped you full of needles and left us with pills and instructions about bathing you when you were fevered and all that. Then he came back to check every few days.

"And Jack said that when you're feeling up to it, we're going to wash your hair. We tried to brush it and keep it nice, but, frankly, Cass, it's a real mess, frizzled and sandy and soaked in salt water. Are you up to it yet?"

Cass sighed. "I think so." She raised her hands to her head. Yes, it was a real mess. It was as it had been when she came out of the sea, and then she had lain with it still wet on the sandy beach. It was caked with grime and salt.

"If you want to get back to your writing, go ahead. I think I'm going to dress today. And then, yes, when Jack comes back, it would be very nice if you would wash my hair."

"All right." Judy waggled her fingers as she left. "Ta-ta."

Cass picked out denim shorts and a light shirt. Her underclothes and socks were in the drawer, and her sneakers were lying by the bed. Once she was dressed again, she began to feel almost normal.

When the men came back, Digger led her into the small bathroom and had her kneel on the mat with her head over the tub. Judy was with him, in charge of handing him shampoo and towels. He squirted shampoo on her head, and with the hand-held shower, temperature carefully tested, went to work on her hair. He rubbed it gently, working the foam into the lumps and snarls, then rinsed it out, being careful to keep the water from going into her ears or onto her face, and untangled some of the snarls with his fingers.

"Can you handle another wash?" he asked, when he had rinsed out the first shampoo. "It really is awful, but if you're tired, I'll quit now."

"Just one more," she said. "Make it a fast one."

Even two weeks ago, the idea that having her hair washed would cause major fatigue would have been unthinkable. But it was true. After the second wash and rinse, she couldn't get up from the floor by herself. Digger wrapped a towel around her dripping hair, then lifted her up and carried her to the bed.

He shifted himself up beside her. "Here," he said, "just slide over in front of me and lean back." He lifted while she squirmed, until she was in front of him, cross-legged, leaning back against his chest.

He unwrapped the towel from around her head, drying gently, starting at the ends and working up the scalp, until the water no longer dripped.

"Judy," he called, "bring me the dryer and hair brush, will you?"

She mugged for them. "Yes, doctor," she said. "Whatever you want, doctor. Scalpel? Tongs?"

He laughed and threw the soggy towel at her.

She took the towel and brought the brush and the cordless dryer, and handed them to Digger. Digger left the dryer untouched at first as he carefully probed the worst tangles, the ones he hadn't been able to smooth while he washed and rinsed her hair, working with the brush, from the ends of each matted knot, unsnarling the hairs without pulling. Twice he muttered about scissors and cutting out the cluster, but each time he worked a little longer, and eventually the hair tangle was removed.

When the tangles were all out, he picked up the dryer. He held it in his right hand, and with his left, lifted and shaped the hair as it dried. When he had it dry, he brushed it carefully, until it slipped, straight and clean and shiny, like tawny gold between his fingers, but she was asleep again long before that, leaning against his chest, head dropped forward.

The next day Digger took Cass to the beach, where she sat on a lounge chair, watching the dolphins, but not going into the water. The dolphins were all there: Joan, and Darby, and little Bubbles. Bugsy was there too, snatching fish and swimming angrily away. The painted pelican cruised the water, parallel to the beach.

Cass dozed in the sun, contented, and Digger sat at her feet. The best of all possible worlds, as the philosopher had said.

Day by day, her strength improved. She knew that she should do something about contacting Carl, about leaving, about getting back to work, but it was so pleasant to just lie in the sun and hold hands with Digger, to watch as her arms and legs once more became strong and golden.

Digger had made the airline arrangements while she was ill, so that her ticket would be good at a later date.

It was easy to sit in the sun and procrastinate, but it wasn't right.

She had to give Digger up. She had to. It wasn't fair to him not to. If she stayed here, she'd be his dependent. At this point, he'd be willing to accept that, but she knew herself too well. She would never be content as a housewife in a trailer. By nine o'clock in the morning she'd have the place shining. Then she'd play with the dolphins for an hour. Then she'd do what? Drive Digger crazy because he'd sense her unhappiness. All the love in the world couldn't overcome a personal sense of uselessness.

Children? Maybe. But she'd have to have a dozen before she'd be busy enough to make it her only career. She'd have to give him up so that he could find a nice girl who'd be contented in a two-bedroom mobile with nothing else to do. The only way she could possibly give him up was to just leave, but she kept pushing it out of her mind.

"I'm still recovering," she told herself. "I have to lie here in the sun until I'm completely recovered."

When she was strong enough she went back to running first thing in the morning. When she finished running, she'd go to the beach and stretch out on the jetty, soaking up the sunshine, healing her body and blanking her mind. At some point, Digger would come join her. Their relationship had become very comfortable. Digger occasionally reached out and took her hand, but otherwise didn't touch her. When she thought about it she told herself that, as head ranger, he didn't really want to lie about necking in the daytime in full sight of his staff.

Generally, she didn't think about it much. Her healing body was concerned with eating and with soaking up the sun. She was content to sit in the sun, close to him, with her hand in his.

At lunchtime, they'd eat in a caravan, either his or

hers. After that she'd sleep through the heat of the afternoon while Digger went back to work. Sometimes in the evening, they would walk or drive for a couple of hours, and she suspected that, after this, Digger spent long hours into the night doing the office work that he neglected, for her, during the day. He was still putting in his forty-hour week, scheduled around her needs and wants. She had no doubt of that.

Cass lay on the jetty, eyes closed, waiting for Digger. She heard footsteps behind her.

"Hi," she said.

"Hi. Why don't we go for a drive?"

The way he said it meant something momentous on the way. Had the time come? He'd said early on that they'd vacation, get to know each other again, and let things happen. Had the time come that Digger had finally decided to say either *Will you marry me?* or *So long, see you around*?

They walked to his car, then drove in silence until he had turned onto the road leading to the shell beach. Still in silence, they drove up it. She was afraid to rush fate by asking what was going on. Digger seemed determined to take his time.

"I thought this would be a nice quiet place," he said as he parked on the red soil overlooking the beach and the ocean.

"It's time, Cass," he said. "Time to plan our future. After we've decided we have one, of course."

She waited.

"I love you, Cass. I want to marry you."

Cass gave a deep and heartfelt sigh. "I love you too," she said. "I always have. When we were in Los Angeles. When I turned down your proposal then. During all years we were apart. I dated other men, but I wasn't attracted to anyone. All I could think of was how feeble they looked when I compared them to you."

"And?"

"And I took up running and sewing and gourmet cooking to fill up my life. I had dinner parties for people I'd known at school and kept in touch with."

His voice hardened. "That's not what I meant when I said 'And.' I meant 'and, now that you've admitted to loving me, will you marry me?' "

"I don't know," she said. "I've been thinking about it and thinking about it and thinking about it. I love you. I want to marry you. But will it all backfire three years down the road? When I'm bored and frustrated will I still be able to make you happy?"

"Explain. Why will you be bored and frustrated three years down the road?"

"Well," she said, "in a way we're back in Los Angeles, aren't we? You wanted me to give up my life and join you. At that time, my education was my life. Now I can't be a complete person unless a career is at least part of my life. Not necessarily the career I have waiting back in Los Angeles. But a career. What will I do here? I'll cook you a gourmet breakfast, and after you've left for work spend ten minutes getting the trailer—mobile—caravan—whatever—spotless. Then I'll run for an hour and play with the dolphins for another hour and come back and make you a gourmet lunch. After lunch, I'll read or watch TV, then cook you a gourmet dinner. Within three years, you'll be fat, and I'll be bored. I don't think there's even any charity work that needs done in the area."

She watched the little ripples beside his jaw. "You're saying you're too good for this hick village, and that being married to me isn't enough for you? Even though you love me so much?"

"No. That's not what I'm saying. I love Dolphin Bay. I could live here happily for the next hundred years if I had useful work to do. As for your next question—if the shoe were on the other foot, would it be enough for you? What if? What if I had an absolutely fantastic career in Los Angeles and we got married and lived in my condo? What if you couldn't find work there? Would you still think that my love would be enough? That you'd be happy getting meals and waiting for me to come home at night?"

"But that's different."

"What's different about it? Think about it, Digger." She leaned her head against the doorpost of the car and closed her eyes.

"So," he said, "the answer's *no*."

"Find me useful work, Digger. Just find me useful

work, and I'll be happy to live with you here forever and with whatever children we may have."

Suddenly she was tired, bone-tired. Her body had not quite returned to normal, after all. She was much too tired to think about it all right now. Life without Digger was unthinkable, but so was life confined to cleaning and cooking. The euphoria of being in love would get her happily through the first two years. But what happened then? She might be madly in love, but she was also a realist.

"I'm tired," she said. "Take me home. I'll think about it and we'll talk again."

Two days later, Cass and Judy sat in Cass's trailer, drinking their afternoon tea. Judy sat at one side of the table, her left leg tucked up under her, her elbows on the table. Cass envied Judy's mop of red curls, her clear greenish-gray eyes, her vixen face. She sighed. She even envied her freckles.

Most of all, she envied her happy marriage.

Cass pushed a plate of chocolate chip cookies toward Judy. "Have a cookie," she said. "When I'm unhappy I cook."

Judy sampled a cookie then laid it on a paper serviette. "Would it be selfish of me to wish you much unhappiness?"

Cass laughed.

Judy took another bite of the cookie and shrugged. "I don't care if it is selfish," she said. "I love chocolate-chip cookies. Seriously, what's the unhappiness about? I had the feeling you didn't invite me over to exchange recipes."

"It's Digger," Cass said. "He asked me to marry him again. I don't know what to do."

Judy shrugged. "No one but you can answer that. Do you love him?"

"Yes. I love him so much I don't feel like a complete person unless he's there. He's such a good person. His love for the dolphins. The way he cared for me when I had pneumonia. The way my heart races whenever he touches me. It's like a firestorm going through. When I'm near him, I can't even breathe because his very presence takes the oxygen from my body."

"So. What's holding you back?"

Cass traced patterns with her finger in her serviette. "There's no career here for me," she said. "You're a woman. I wanted to talk to you because I thought you'd understand."

Judy paused. "I guess it was easier for me," she said. "I was a teacher, and teaching jobs exist almost everywhere. Jon told me I could teach or not, as I chose. He said he'd share the housework. He didn't ask me to choose between marriage and a career. But then, my book sold, and so did the next one, and I decided I'd give up teaching for writing. It's worked out. Has Digger asked you to choose?"

"No. But it's a matter of location. Jon lived and

worked in Boston. Don't get me wrong. I love it here. But there's nothing for me. He can't give me a job because it would be nepotism. There aren't any other jobs here remotely connected with what I trained for."

"Well," Judy said, "I guess that's harder. Sometimes these things just work themselves out. Maybe you could help in the visitors' center on a volunteer basis. You know a lot about dolphins. Then, there's the school. I'm sure the teachers would love a volunteer, especially in the science classes. With your background you could really bring science to life. You could drive over and ask if that's a possibility. Maybe you could collect data on dolphins. Take some of the stuff Digger's collected, but doesn't have time to write up. Or compile a dolphin bibliography for visitors who want to find out more. You can get the information you need on the computer now. Just some ideas."

"Guess I need to think a little harder than I was."

"It's your decision, Cass, but based on my own marriage, and on the way you and Digger look at each other, I'd say, never let him go."

"Thanks," Cass said fervently. "Thanks. I won't."

Cass bought groceries and, from her memory, wrote down the details of some of her favorite meals.

Roast lamb, she'd make for him. Prove to him that she could be a true Australian. Judy had promised to smuggle her over a Pavlova. Cass knew she'd be capable of doing it herself, but Judy was proud of her one culinary specialty.

Meal planned, and trailer spotless, she put on the yellow sundress she'd worn in Los Angeles, and faced Digger in his office.

"Dinner tonight?" she said. "Or *tea*, if you'd rather call it that. I'll see you promptly at six-thirty. I've something to tell you."

He appeared right on time. She served stuffed mushrooms before the meal, then roast lamb with mint and small potatoes and green peas. Her dinner rolls were homemade.

She asked him about his work and the dolphins and told him that, yes, she felt better now and was running further each day.

Over tea and Pavlova, she finally looked at him and said, "I've been thinking. And I had a chat with Judy. Sometimes it helps to have a sounding board."

"And what was this chat with Judy all about?"

"You. She told me I'd be crazy if I let a good catch like you get away."

Digger chuckled. "You agreed?"

"Oh, yes," she said. "I've made up my mind. If you'll marry me, I'll live here with you in your caravan, and if a cyclone blows it away, I'll live with you here in a tent, and we'll have a million babies who'll run naked on the beach and swim with the wild dolphins."

"And what about all this boredom?"

"When I get too bored, I'll see if the local school will let me volunteer."

"Well," he said, "the tent probably won't be necessary, and we can probably reduce the number of babies from a million to two or three. Otherwise, it sounds like a plan. Now, finish your tea and let's go for a drive. I've been thinking too. I thought about you asking me if I'd be happy doing nothing but keeping house for you. Now, I understand better, and I've had an idea."

They drove into the village. Digger stopped on the outskirts, and parked in front of a vacant house with a "for sale" sign on the lawn.

"I didn't mean I wanted a house, Digger. I don't mind living in your trailer. Not for a while, anyway."

"That's not what I was thinking of. Just look at it. Do you like it?"

The house took her breath away. It was a Victorian house, built by someone a hundred years or so ago, in the days when families had thirteen kids and servants and money to match. The things she could do with a place like this, given the money. She'd paint it all white, and then the gingerbread, under the eaves, ah, the gingerbread—

She snapped her attention away from the house. Digger was talking. "See. It's a real old Australian house, with a real old Australian verandah for sitting and talking on warm evenings. Anyway, it's going cheap. I've checked it out, and it's structurally sound.

It would need a lot of renovating, but it doesn't all have to be done at once."

She looked at him intently, wondering what a really big Australian house, even if she did really love it, could possibly have to do with her independence. Then she forgot everything else in looking into his blue eyes, watching the lock of blond hair that tumbled down onto his forehead, drowning in the light of his smile. Just as she'd told Judy, the air left her lungs with a swoosh and her legs turned to jelly. She breathed deeply to recover.

"Go on," she said.

"My idea is that we'll buy it. We'll live in the caravan for now, but we can work on the house evenings and weekends, as we get time and money. When we get the kitchen, living area, and one bedroom done, we'll move in. Then, when we finish another bedroom, we'll start advertising for tourists—but not just any tourists. We want real dolphin aficionados, influential people, and politicians. They'll stay for two weeks or more, and will be immersed in dolphins. We'll have a dolphin library, and dolphin videos. You'll give them lectures on dolphins and bring them to the beach personally."

"Aren't you being a bit elitist? Influential people and politicians?"

"No. First, Dolphin Bay already has the campground for tourists. But there are two other reasons. One is that for the first few years, we aren't going to be able to take many at a time. So we need ones willing and able to pay enough to make this worth your while and to pay as much as possible of the mortgage. Also, the dolphins, and all wild things, need protection, so we want to target the people who will go back and legislate that protection or contribute generously to organizations dedicated to their protection.

"Now, you're a gourmet cook, so you can also make this a special place that way. Hopefully, we'll soon be able to afford help for you so that all your time can be spent in dolphin education rather than on household chores. If I do other trips like the one to LA, you'll come with me, but otherwise I really want to stay here. I know that we could probably both get teaching jobs in Perth, but I don't want to. If you want it badly, I will, but I want to stay here with the dolphins. I'm going to be doing some research, and you can help me with that. I want to stay."

"Yes," she said. "So do I. It sounds like a grand idea, Digger. I'll help you with research, any way I can, and I think the first-class tourist hotel is a good idea, too. And I don't mind the household chores— really I don't."

"I'll pitch in and help," he said. "I've been neglecting the office with all this, and I'll be taking a few weeks after the wedding as vacation time so that we can have a honeymoon. After that, I'll have to keep regular hours, but when my work day's over, I will pitch in."

"It won't take as long as you think to get this place on its feet," she said. "I should realize a good profit on the condo and we can use that money to apply on the mortgage. And I've got some savings. I was saving for a car. Carl paid me for some of the weeks and weeks of vacation time I've never taken, so that paid for most of the trip."

"Well," he said, "I've a fair bit saved too. After all, I've been working at this job for several years and there's not exactly a lot of places to spend money here. And the house is going for a really good price. It's been vacant for quite a while, and the owners live in Sydney now. They just want to be rid of it. There's not a lot of demand in Dolphin Bay for Victorian houses. But come on—the real estate people gave me a key. Come on inside."

The key stuck, then turned with a groan. "Needs a shot of oil," Digger said.

They stepped inside and stood in the entry hall. The wallpaper was peeling and the hardwood floors needed sanding and varnishing. But they were hardwood floors.

"The ceilings must be twenty feet high," Cass said. A curving staircase swept down from the second story.

They made a right turn and entered the kitchen. "It's the size of my whole condo," Cass said.

"We'll probably have to strip it and put in all new cabinets."

"Oh, no, you don't," Cass said. "It's perfect. It's

just like those mansions in Victorian novels." She opened some cupboard doors. "I want it left to look like a Victorian kitchen. The cupboards aren't rotting or anything. Sure, we'll have to put in new stoves and wall ovens and fridges for convenience. But for the rest—a good sanding and paint job's all they need." She walked on through. "Here's a huge pantry," she said. "The freezer and an extra fridge can go in here. I'll have a washer and dryer here for the downstairs wash, and another upstairs for the bedrooms." She found her thoughts racing. Next chance she had, she'd buy a bunch of home decorating magazines. She loved this sort of thing.

They moved on. The house had large double parlors as well as a number of smaller dens, libraries, morning rooms, whatever. "We'll take one of these rooms for a bedroom at first," she said. "It shouldn't be too long until we can move in."

She moved to the library window and looked out. The property was large, but the gardens and flowerbeds had been neglected for years. "I'll redo the gardens," she said. "Use native plants as far as possible."

"It'll be awhile before you make much money, you know."

She looked at him. "It's not the money," she said. "I just have to feel a sense of accomplishment." She grinned. "This should give me about ten years' worth of that, even without clients."

"So you'll do it then." He chuckled. "This should

satisfy your desire to work like a man. And you will at first, with hammers and nails and paintbrushes. So, knowing all that, you're in?"

"I'm in," she said.

"When do you want to get married?"

She shrugged, then stood on tiptoe and rubbed her nose against his. "You're the guy who lives here. You know what the rituals are and how long it takes to get a license."

"So I'm in charge? That means it won't be long. I want to get married right away. I'm thirty, and I've waited for you for six years. I want you in my house and in my life. You'll marry me now, Cass, and be my mate?"

"Yes," she said. She wrapped both arms around his waist, and laid her cheek against his chest. "Yes. I'll be your sheila if you'll be my bloke."

"So. Any requirements for this wedding?"

"Just one," she said. "I want to get married on the beach. Do you think you could make the tourists wait or something that day, so that we can have the beach to ourselves for an hour or so? *They* might come to my wedding."

She felt tears sliding down her face and wiped them away. "This is silly," she said. "I hardly ever cry, and when I do, I don't let anybody else see me. And why now, when I'm so happy?"

He put out a forefinger and touched the tears. "It

means we belong together, Cass. We share. You'll never have to cry by yourself again."

"And I can have my wedding on the beach?"

"On the beach. On a boat. In an airplane. Wherever you want. And, yes, I'll just ask the rangers to tell the tourists what's going on, and ask them to wait. I guess on the beach means a small wedding, doesn't it?"

"Sort of small. Judy and Jon. I want Judy to be my bridesmaid. And if Carl and MaryAnne could get away. I'll phone Mom and Dad. Maybe my sister, but they both work, so there's not much chance. Then there's your family. And probably some of the people you work with."

Digger chuckled and rolled his eyes. "The typical small wedding that gets out of hand. You'll have to phone the ones in America right away. I'll find a minister in the village. As I remember you made some promises to God about church, so we might as well go that route." He paused. "And I suppose a stretch limousine and a thousand white doves."

She snapped him on the nose with her middle finger, but he just grabbed it and nibbled it.

"Okay," he said, "that was a joke." He got a dreamy far away look in his blue eyes. "And a white dress. Beach or no beach—a long white dress, all lace and satin. A true wedding dress for my bride."

"So," Digger said as they sat on the beach the next afternoon, "you told me there's never been anyone else you were serious about." He dribbled sand over her shoulders. "Was that the truth?"

"Well," Cass said, "there was a fellow about six years ago. He was tall and blond and handsome. He came to me from the Australian desert, over the Pacific, leaping the waves like a dolphin. That was the first and last man I ever loved. Every night, I saw him in my dreams."

He tried to chuckle. "Well, Cass," he said, "that might have provided a most satisfactory love life for you, but it didn't do a lot for the poor bloke from Australia."

His eyes were wet, she saw, just before his mouth came down on hers and blotted out everything else for them both.

Epilogue

They stood on the beach, the minister in his black clerical robes with his back to the water, the wedding party standing in front of him facing the water. The few wedding guests—Digger's family, Cass's parents, Carl and MaryAnne and their youngest child, and a few of the rangers—sat in folding plastic chairs behind the wedding party. The wedding party was also small, just Digger and Cass, Jon and Judy, and Carl's oldest daughter, who with a poise beyond her years, held Cass's little nosegay of garden flowers while the rings were exchanged, and then gave it back to her.

"I now pronounce you man and wife," the minister said, and Digger bent to kiss his bride.

"Oh," she gasped, moving away from him, pointing out into the bay. "There they are. They've come." She

179

looked up at Digger. "Oh, Digger, the dolphins have come to my wedding."

She grasped the sides of her white gown and hoisted it up far enough to be out of the water, kicked off her white pumps, and waded in, Digger close behind her, his rented tuxedo wet to the knees, his hand resting on her waist. The dolphins swam by in a slow procession, Joan and Bugsy and Bubbles and Darby at the end.

Joan swam up and touched Cass with her beak. Bugsy gave her a long look. He didn't touch her, but Cass could have sworn he winked at her before he moved away. Then Darby nosed Bubbles up to be patted, and Cass clutched her gown with one hand and reached down and scratched the baby's beak with the other. Darby touched Cass with her beak, resting it on the blue garter just above Cass's knee, a long and lingering touch, almost a caress, and a deep feeling of peace and well being flowed from the dolphin into Cass.

Darby had blessed her. Digger rested his hand on the small of her back, his strength and love flowing into her too.

She turned to him, her free hand moving to his face. Then she let go of the dress completely, leaving it awash in the salt water rising to her knees, so she could move both arms around his neck.

"Oh," she said as she realized, "I'm still holding my

bouquet. I was supposed to throw it away. Isn't that bad luck or something?"

Digger laughed. "No, honey," he said. "It's just that whoever catches it will be the next to marry. Considering that all the women present are either happily married or under six, I would think it would have been worse luck to throw it.

"Why don't you just throw it to the dolphins?" he added. "There isn't any wire or anything like that in it, is there?"

"No," she said. "It's just a little nosegay of garden flowers and a length of paper ribbon." She swung the bouquet in an arc, sending it far out into the water.

She saw the first dolphin catch it and fling it into the air, and another one toss it forward, and the school raced down the bay, playing with the flowers, making their happy dolphin sounds.

She turned to Digger again, drinking in his strength and goodness, his tenderness for her—her love and her luck filled her heart until it seemed that it would burst.

"Oh, Digger," she said, "I love you so much I can't stand it. I have been twice blessed, by you and by the dolphins. And the dolphins sang at my wedding. Sang their dolphin song." She nodded toward the bay. "I can't stand it—so much happiness, so much blessing."

He looked down at her, at the trace of tears trembling on her lashes, at the glow that transformed her face. His voice was husky. "We're both blessed, Cass.

Blessed by the dolphins, and by each other—and by fate."

"By the dolphins, by each other—and by the fate that led me to you and Dolphin Bay." She raised her face to his to complete the interrupted kiss.

His mouth claimed hers, fulfilling the promise of the wedding vows, and she clung to him so closely that it seemed as if she were trying to merge her very soul with his.

Out in the bay, the sun sparkled on the blue waves and the dolphins frolicked to and fro, playing ringtoss with her bridal flowers.